Whammo Ranch

by
Jerry Boyd

This book is a work of fiction. All the people, events, and organizations in this book are products of the author's imagination. Any resemblance to anything in the real world is purely coincidental

Copyright©2019 Jerry Boyd

Nikki and I were enjoying the sunshine and playing Frisbee with Snitz. He was getting better at catching. Being part Border Collie must help. Max, Nikki's dad, came running out of the house, hollering, "Bob, come quick, we've got a saucer coming in and it sounds bad."

I asked, "Medical or mechanical?"

"Both, I think. The guy on the communicator seems awfully flustered. Can't really get a good report out of him."

I caught Snitz, and put his leash on. I handed it to Max and told him, "Take him in the house so he doesn't run off again. We'll get the garage ready."

I turned to Nikki and asked, "Space Cadet, can you please move that jalopy the pirates flew in on down to the barn? I'll get the doors for you."

I ran and started the garage door up, and then ran down to the barn to open that door. When I got it folded back out of the way, I got out my phone to call my partner, John.

"Hey, John, you folks about done over there? We've got company coming, and Max thinks they want to talk to you."

"We just got back from looking at the pond. I'll tell you about it later. Any idea what these folks need?"

"Max says they're pretty rattled, he hasn't gotten much good info."

"I'll let Dee drive. We'll get there quicker."

"Brave man, see you soon."

I went in the house and got a couple of those nice stun rifles we salvaged the other week. When I got to the garage, I made sure there was a pair of nice, big extinguishers handy. A saucer coming in on fire is no fun.

Nikki got back from the barn, and I handed her a stunner. She looked concerned, and asked, "You think we need these, Caveman?"

"After last time, I'd rather have them than not."

"Good point."

I got out my communicator, so I could shut down their drive when they touched down. I was feeling pretty paranoid, after getting a visit from the pirates. Just about then, Max yelled from the house, "They're coming in!"

I noticed Nikki had a scanner out, but whatever my new wife was worried about, she would let me know when I needed to. I heard the saucer touch down, and killed their drive. I hit the button to run the door down, to keep anyone from seeing what we had parked here. When I turned around, Nikki was shouting into her communicator, "Stay in the vehicle! Do! Not! Open the door!" Nikki approached the saucer door, and slapped on a device I hadn't seen before. She said, "That will hold for now, but we need some help in here, as soon as we can get it."

"More pirates?"

"Much worse. They're carrying one of the most deadly diseases we know of. If they had opened the saucer, this whole planet would have been at risk."

I heard gravel bouncing off the garage door. "Dee's here!"

We went outside to tell the others what was going on. Nikki said, "Grandpa, it's the Bethene flu. I sealed the ship, but what should we do next?"

"Bethene flu? Don't all Guide ships carry vaccine and antivirals that work?"

"I'm not here in a Guide ship. I was guiding a study party in their vehicle."

"So my ship is the only Guide vessel on the planet?"

"As far as I know, it is, Grandpa."

"Have you called the Patrol yet?"

"I was about to when it started raining rocks."

Dee said, "John said to hurry. Sideways is fast."

Dingus said,"Don't worry, Granddaughter, I'll call the Patrol. This local bunch seems to have an attitude problem."

Dingus got out his communicator called them up. I wandered over to talk to John. "Assuming the Patrol tells us to piss up a rope, Dingus' saucer is our only shot. How bad is getting it out gonna be?"

"The mud in the bottom of that pond is some sticky crap. Breaking the suction is not going to be easy."

Dingus was cussing in English, Spanish, his language, and at least a couple more languages I didn't know. The person on the other end of the communicator was apparently not impressed, as he was hung up on. "Silly bastard says he doesn't care who the scanner says I am, it must have been faked somehow. They don't believe there is any Bethene flu, and even if there was, it's our problem."

Trying to avoid aggravating Dingus any further, I asked, "Is there a Guide post anywhere close?"

"I'm not sure these days. Nikki, how far out are we?"

"Two days hard flying. I'll give them a call. No need trying to verify your ID over the comm."

"This is guide Benikkious Slongum, ID # AZ3487-VQ9247-PK7623, can you verify?"

She had put it on speaker. "Your identification is verified, Ensign. How can I help you today?"

"Sir, we have Bethene flu, and no supplies to deal with it. We may be able to obtain some, but that is unsure at this time. Victims are quarantined, and have not had contact with locals. Can you aid us?"

"Isn't there a Patrol base nearer to you than we are?"

"They refuse to help, claiming they don't believe it is Bethene flu. They also doubt the identification of my Grandfather, who has been found and woken from suspension."

"Dingolus is alive!? After all this time? I remember seeing a recording of one of his speeches at the academy. We'll send out a medical unit, with equipment to prove Dingolus' identity beyond doubt. Even our fastest ship will be two days."

"I know sir. As I said, the plague ship is under quarantine, I put an exterior lock over the hatch."

"Good thinking, Ensign. Good luck."

I asked, "Exterior lock? Wouldn't that have been handy with the pirates?"

"Sure would've, Caveman. They had the door open before I had a chance to place it."

"That answers that. Figured there was a good reason. Do you think all three of the loader robots will fit in the back of my truck?"

"It'll be tight, but they're made to collapse for transit. What evil plan is cranking in that Caveman brain?"

"There's medicine on your Granddad's saucer. All we have to do is raise it."

"Pull a multi-ton saucer out of a hundred years of mud, that's all, huh?"

"Nobody ever said it wasn't gonna be semi-tough."

Nikki fiddled with her watch. "That's got to be another one of your silly movie references. Oh. Here it is. What is it with Burt Reynolds? The doctor who delivered you have a mustache or something?"

We went in to eat, and wait for dark, since saucers and hi tech cargo bots are not something you want to be seen with, here on Earth.

"Hey, John, I've got a portable compressor over at the old place, runs on gas. Do you think we could rig a pipe to pump air into the mud and loosen Dingus' ride?"

"Might be worth a shot. With three bots lifting, it might break loose. I've got some half inch black pipe, have you got fittings to hook it up?"

"I think so. Could you trade me keys, Nikki? You guys will need my truck to haul bots."

"Sure, Bob. Careful with it, it's my first car."

"Space Cadet, I know you let Dee drive it, don't give me that crap."

I ran into town, hoping to be back by dark. How my old neighbor always knows when I'm coming into town, I'll never know, but there he was, waving at me. Of course, I had to stop and chat.

"Hey, how's it going?"

"Good, Bob, and you?"

"Got married yesterday, so pretty darn good right now."

"Married!? Where's Bob Wilson, and what did you do with him?"

"Still me, Joshua, still me. Just found the right lady and didn't want to give her the chance to wise up."

"Best of luck to both of you."

"Thanks, sorry, gotta go."

I grabbed everything that looked like it could be useful in saucer raising, and headed out to my farm, where the pond was. Need to get moved in one of these days. Hopefully this week. John was waiting for me at the house, since I didn't know where the pond was. "Do you think we can get this thing out of the mud, John?"

"If we put steady pressure on it, and use your air pipe, I think we have a shot. If we have to wait for the Guides to get here, I'm not sure we can help the people on that saucer. We need to get supplies of this, to keep on hand. Probably other stuff we need to have handy, too. I need to take some more training, find out about medical techniques they have that we don't."

"All that salvage the Patrol let us have is going to help a lot, but I need to get a parts inventory built up. Not every problem is going to be as easy to fix as the ones we've had so far."

"Do we really have any business trying to do all this?"

"If it wasn't for us, there would be no help for travelers out this way. Two dumb hillbillies beats the snot out of nobody."

"You're right, but I still feel like we may have bitten off more than we can chew."

"You and me both. Feels like we're riding a mean old Brahma, and the clock stopped at six seconds. Where's the clown, I wanna get off."

"You hit the nail on the head. You manage to project calm so well, I didn't think you were worried."

"Not worried? I just married an alien. Dee's rejuve is gonna make it impossible for her to use her old ID. I can't even find time to move into this nice old house I bought. What do I have to worry about? Some crazy space plague infecting the planet? Come on, John, the last month or so has been nuts, I just haven't had the free time to get drunk and freak out about it."

"We have met some cool people, though. Dee was a hoot even before Dingus put her in the box and made her young again. I mean, Dingus, how often are you going to meet an alien gunfighter who's been asleep since the old west. Lyla, the alien crime reporter, she's gonna make her career with the Dingus' story. Even Max, the alien worrywart."

"Not to mention Nikki. If she had gotten her saucer back in the air before I got home, none of this would have happened. We would still be broke, trying to figure out how to stay sane. All of this is nuts, and I keep expecting somebody to show up with a little flashy thing and take it all away, but I don't want to have to go back to how things were."

"Me either. Let's get the saucer out of the mud, and save the day again."

"Keep it up, Dee's going to get us capes."

We got back to the pond. The others were getting the robots unloaded and positioned around the saucer, except for Lyla, who was filming the whole operation for her story. I got the pipe out of the truck and built a stinger long enough to reach the center of the pond. I put an air fitting on the end of it, and started the compressor. Once we had pressure, I hooked up the stinger, and started to work it under the saucer. At first all I got was bubbles, but soon enough it got a seal and started to lift. Everything was good until the air bubble under the saucer finally broke out. Hundred year old mud is never going to be a popular fragrance. John said, "Bob, that's worse than your chili farts. Wish I would have thought to bring a gas mask."

Dingus got on his communicator at this point, and started driving the bots. He had them swish the saucer back and forth in the pond, trying to wash off some mud. Then he maneuvered them around so they wouldn't have to go through the pond to get the saucer on solid ground. They sat it down, and I used a blowgun nozzle to try and clean up around the door. Dingus gave up and wiped the access panel with his shirtsleeve. Once he was inside, he called out, "Everybody stand back!"

He did something, and all the mud just fell off. Gotta get one of those for my truck. A few moments later, he came racing out with an armload of stuff, saying, "John, help me load this stuff, we need to get back as soon as we can."

They loaded Nikki's truck, and I gave them the keys. Lyla went with them to record the action, and Dee went also, to be with Dingus. Besides, they needed to get back quickly. The sideways is strong with Dee. John, Nikki and I stayed to help the bots get themselves and the saucer under cover before daylight. I was sure that if the government ever had an excuse to run back their satellite records, we would all be in deep trouble, but as long as we could keep a low profile, we might have a chance to keep running 'Bob's Saucer Repair'.

Dingus had used the power core from his saucer to keep his suspension chamber running, so we couldn't just fly it to the barn. Backup power wouldn't get it airborne, and it sure wouldn't engage the stealth field to keep it from showing up on radar. Cargo bots are not designed for overland travel, of course, so we had to take it slow.

Nikki scouted us a nice smooth route, driving ahead of us. She got a call. Dingus had forgotten to get the cancel code for the lock she put on the plague saucer. We started moving again, and got the saucer inside. The bots did their creepy contortionist folding routine again on the truck, and we tarped them down and headed back to John's. When we got there, Dee and Lyla were standing outside the garage. It was sealed up with plastic and duct tape. Dee announced, "Dingus said nobody gets in 'til he calls the all clear, or the Guide shows up. This means you, Bob Wilson!"

I held up my hands in surrender, "No problem. I'm going to bed. Come get me if you need to."

Nikki and I went in the house to get Snitz, and then we wandered down to the barn, to sleep in her saucer.

Entirely too soon, Snitz licked my ear. Apparently it was time to check and make sure no one had made off with his outdoors while we slept. After seeing that all was well, and taking care of some business, we walked up to the house to see if there was coffee to be had. Dee was in the kitchen, making magical smells. She said, "There's coffee in the pot there, Zombie Bob."

I lifted my arms straight out, and moaned, "Coffee!"

After a few sips of the elixir of life, I was able to ask, "What's the word from plague central?"

"Dingus and John say they got to those people in time, but it will be a while before they are well enough to drop the quarantine. They are both busy decontaminating the saucer and the garage. Dingus thinks they may be able to open up before the Guide shows up, but he's not sure yet."

"Did he get back with them and tell them the situation was under control?"

"He did, but they're all psyched up about meeting the famous Dingolus Slongum. I guess he was really somebody, back in the day."

"Still is, if you ask me."

"You got that right. Ooh, that man!"

"Enough, Dee, I don't wanna know."

I had some breakfast, and grabbed another cup of coffee to take to Nikki. Dee said, "Domesticated already, isn't it wonderful?"

"Just interested in self preservation. Have you seen Nikki before she gets her coffee?"

When I got back to the saucer, the wonderful aroma of coffee wasn't enough to bring Nikki back to the world of the living. Snitz decided to help. One ear lick is all it takes, instant alertness. "Dammit, dog, I'm sleeping. Get Caveman to take you out."

"Space Cadet, I have coffee."

"You might be worth keeping around, Caveman."

Once Nikki got rid of some of the blood in her caffeine system, we went back up to the house. Max was sitting on the porch. Snitz ran to him. I said, "If I'm not careful, he's gonna wind up your dog, as much time as you spend with him."

"As long as saucers put out the noise that scares him, it's gotta be that way, Bob.", Nikki said.

Max said, "I can think of worse things.".

I replied, "At least you're not scared of the domesticated wolf, anymore."

"Your world is a lot different than where I come from."

"You seem to be picking it up quick enough. Do you have any ideas on what to charge these people for bringing plague into our lives?"

"We actually got lucky when the Patrol refused to help. They would have charged us, and we would have had to pass that cost along. The Guides are mostly just coming to see Dingolus, and if they need to help out, they will. We can't really charge them for raising Dad's saucer, we were going to do that anyway. We can't evaluate the condition of their vehicle until the quarantine is lifted, so that's still a mystery. I'm pretty lost, how about you?"

"They definitely have occupied our facility, to the exclusion of any other use, and we certainly can charge for Dingus' and John's time, and whatever supplies they used. I feel like we ought to put on a hefty surcharge for landing without telling us they had a contagious disease aboard."

"I see your point, but I'm not sure how to make that sound businesslike on a bill."

"We'll think of something. Can't have people thinking we're pushovers. Have you heard anything from the Patrol about that saucer the pirates flew in yesterday? Is that going to be ours, or are they coming for it?"

"Actually, that's why I'm out here. They said they would be here for it soon."

"Nikki, you better take Snitz in the house, we don't want him to run off."

"Okay, you staying to meet them?"

"Might as well. I want to stay around, but there's not much to do right now."

"Hey, Max, do you know anything about getting clear title to those saucers they let us salvage? We can't do much with them if they're not legal."

"I'll check into it and let you know, Bob. I don't have a clue off the top of my head."

Just then I heard Snitz whine from inside the house. The Patrol had arrived. Sergeant Darning stepped out when they landed. "I, uh, got flustered yesterday and forgot to get that saucer. Is it still in the garage?"

"No, we had to move it. Had some paying customers come in, with presents."

"Presents?"

"You didn't hear about the Bethene flu?"

He looked around, somewhat panicked, but the ship that brought him had already left. I said, "It's quarantined, and the patients are receiving treatment. Kind of put us in a bind when you fellas wouldn't help out, but we found some medicine and got things under control."

"We what? I know the Major doesn't like you lot, but that's crazy."

"What's the Major got against us? He seemed friendly enough."

"That kid your wife bounced out of his research was the Major's nephew."

"That explains a lot. Come on, we better get you airborne, before he has an excuse to gig you for being late."

I opened the barn for him. "The stealth was flickering when they came in. I don't know if that was a real issue, or they were trying to convince us they were in trouble."

"Oh, goody. Mind if I run a diagnostic before I leave?"

"Be our guest, just please don't use main power 'til you're ready to leave. We're not sure if us primitives have good enough tech to pick the signature or not, but we'd rather be safe."

"You mean you guys aren't sanctioned by your government?"

"Not at all. If they find out about us, we'll be in dark little cells until they find out everything we know about saucers and you folks."

"I believe your phrase is, 'Big Brass Ones'."

"Hear that a lot, lately."

He ran his diagnostic, and found that the stealth problem was, in fact, a program they had put in place to look worse off than they were. He fired it up, and was gone. I closed the garage, and went back to the house.

The ladies were all sitting around the kitchen table when I got inside. I asked, "Any of you know how to give a shot? I need to train on Dingus' saucer."

Dee spoke up, "I used to give a friend of mine her insulin, when her eyes got too bad to do it herself. I can help you out if you know the right dose."

"John's got it written down. I'll show you."

While we were getting set up, I asked Dee, "We had planned to get you certified competent, and go from there. Since you took rejuve, nobody's going to believe you're the same lady. Do you just want a new ID, or how do you want to handle it?"

"I guess I'm going to have to be somebody new, but I better keep my first name. I don't think I could learn to answer to a new name after all this time."

"We'll take some pictures later. John can send them in when he gets out of quarantine. Any other problems you have with how things are going?"

"No. You fellas have taken wonderful care of me. Sure wish I had that Chevelle back that my son took when he got my license. I feel like a mooch, having to bum a ride."

"No promises, but I'll look into it."

"Thanks, Bob."

When I got done with my class and woke up, I heard the TV running in the other room. The ladies were having a big time. I decided not to bother them and went to find Max. "Hey, Max, I need a little help, if you've got time."

"Sure, Bob, what do you need?"

"You made an inventory of all the stuff we salvaged, didn't you?"

"I did. Looking for something in particular?"

"A power core for your Dad's saucer. I think one of those we couldn't get flying has a core that will work, but I don't remember what kind of shape it was in."

"Let's see, is this the one you were talking about?"

"That's it. This says that core is almost new, I wonder how it wound up in that junker?"

"Probably just what was available. Their operation didn't seem all that well run."

"This says it's an improved model with more power, I need to figure out how many other problems that will cause."

Max showed me how to access the data I needed, and I found a simple software patch that would keep the bigger core from overloading the other parts. I thanked Max, and told him I was going over to my place to get started pulling that core and fixing Dingus' saucer. I hopped a cargo bot in the truck to help with the lifting, and tarped it down. Snitz wanted to come along, and hopped in the truck. When I got to our new place, I had a thought. I called the lawyer John and I had talked to about Delilah's competency hearing. I asked if he could get an investigator to find Dee's old car, and put whatever charges he incurred on our bill. He said he would be glad to. I told him we probably weren't going forward with the hearing, but we would no doubt have other business for him soon. We said our goodbyes, and Snitz and I wandered off to the barn. Getting the power core out of the saucer wasn't nearly as hard as I had feared. Having the bot to hold things up helped immensely. I had a small service bot crawl behind and undo a couple of bolts. I wish I had one of those when I used to work at the dealership. In the process of wrestling the core out of one saucer, and into the other, I found a few places that looked as if they might be vibrating against one another. I had a piece of inner tube in the truck's toolbox, and used it to cushion those spots. Once the core was snugged up in Dingus' saucer, I tried to get in to run diagnostics. The saucer threatened to stun me, so I backed off and called Dingus. "Are you busy right now, Dingus?"

"No, Bob, we're just passing time waiting for all the virus to be gone from these folks' systems. I can send the diagnostic report to your communicator if you would like."

"That would be great, I can find the parts they need and have them ready. I called about something else, though. I put a new power core in your saucer for you, but I can't get in to run diagnostics on it."

"Bob, you're a wonder! Where did you get a core?"

"One of those saucers we couldn't get running the other night had a nearly new core that would fit. Just lucky, it seems."

"When I hang up, I'll tell the saucer to give you maintenance access. That's all I can do from here. You can run diagnostics and check systems, but if you try to take off, it won't let you."

"Sounds good, thanks."

By the time the diagnostic finished, it was suppertime. A few problems had shown up, but I could deal with those tomorrow. I left the bot, in case I had more heavy parts to move tomorrow. Snitz and I climbed in the truck and drove back. When we got in the house, Dee said, "I told you he would be back for supper. He may be dumb, but he likes to eat."

"What thanks I get for working on your man's ride all afternoon!"

Nikki jumped in, "Ooh, Bob is doing his job, all hail Bob. Wash up for supper, Caveman."

I said, "Max, have I ever thanked you for raising her to be so kind and respectful?"

"No, Bob, you haven't."

"There's a reason for that."

After supper, Max and I made a list of parts I needed to get from the other place to be ready to fix our customer's saucer when the quarantine was lifted. I asked, "I keep calling them 'our customers'. Do we have a name for these folks?"

"Dad says they claim to be Mister and Missus Duram, and their son Hirus. Duram is like Smith or Jones in your culture, so he is a little suspicious."

"Any way to check that?"

"The Patrol has a database. Getting them to help is the problem."

"Do we have Sergeant Darn-Your-Socks' private comm code?"

"We do, you sneaky primitive."

"Hook me up, we'll see if he's willing to help."

"Sergeant Darning, how are you this fine day?"

"Bob Wilson. I tremble in fear over what this call could be about."

"Oh now, Mike, the Major's still in quarantine, he's not going to shoot your ass today."

"Not today, you say?"

"The week's still young, Mike. Could you possibly run a couple of IDs for us? These folks that brought us the flu seem a little hinky."

"Hinky? Oh, I see, one of your colloquialisms. You don't think they're who they say they are?"

"Mr. and Mrs. Duram, would you risk a half ounce on that?"

"No, Bob, I would not."

I sent him what data we had. He came back immediately. "You boys do love your bounties, don't you? Let me know when they get out of quarantine, I'll have to come get them."
"They are traveling with a minor child, just so you are aware."
"That does complicate things."
"What about their saucer? It needs repairs before it's airworthy, will the Patrol pay for that?"
"I doubt it. You could, however, bid on transporting it to our base."
"Okay. While I've got you, I need to ask about another little thing. How do we go about getting good title to these salvage vehicles, so we can operate them legally?"
"I'll send you the forms. It's just a formality, in this case, since the Patrol directed you to take them."
"I hope you're right. Thanks."
I forwarded the forms to Max, since he handled all the paperwork. "Max, please, see if there's a way for the Patrol Major to hold us up on those, and do all you can to see that he doesn't."
"I'll do what I can, Bob. We may need to file in a different district."
"Would you need to do that in person?"
"Could be. Let me see if I can get someone to handle it for us."
It was getting late. I called John to check in before I called it a night. "Hi, Bob, what's up?"
"Nothing, really. Just checking in to see how it's going."
"Pretty good. We should be able to unseal in the morning."
"That's great! Can you call me before you do that, though? I need to make some arrangements."
"This about what Dingus and Max discussed?"
"It is. We have another lucky winner. Watch yourself, they probably have weapons stashed."
"I see what you're saying, Robert. I'll take care of that for you."
"See you in the morning, then."
I shouted, "Everybody gear up. I think Dingus and John have been taken hostage."
Max asked, "Why do you say that?"
"John called me Robert. He never does that unless he's trying to signal me about something."
"Should we call the Patrol?"
I said, "Not until we're sure."

We just got off the porch when the garage door started up. All of us took up firing positions, even Max. A man came into view, holding a weapon to Dingus' head. He was hit with five stunner bolts before he could speak. I heard a commotion inside the garage, and John yelled, "I've got her, but the kid is still in the saucer."

Dingus looked a little loopy, from being so close to all those stunner hits, but he was still standing. Dee went to help him. Nikki and I went to clear the saucer, while Lyla and Max covered the prisoners. I called out, "Okay, kid, no need for any more trouble. Come on out, and we'll get all this sorted out."

"I'm scared. You're going to hurt me."

"No, we're not. I'm coming in now, just stay calm."

I walked through the door. I felt the pain, I felt myself falling. I heard Nikki yell, and I heard her stunner go off. A lot.

When I woke up, I was confused, because I had never been in the autodoc before. Nikki and John were looking down at me. Nikki said, "You stupid S.O.B., why didn't you wait for a flash bang? That little twerp almost killed you. Don't ever do that to me again!"

"You're right. I was stupid. He sounded so scared, I just didn't think."

John said, "Well, we got you in here quick enough, this time. That's enough stupid John Wayne stunts, you hear!?"

"Yes, John, I hear. Is the plague contained?"

"They were clear before the excitement. We were just trying to keep them contained 'til we could get word to you to be ready."

"Anybody call the Patrol? Apparently the two adults have bounties."

"They've been and gone. Brought us titles to all the saucers we salvaged. Dingus called in a favor, and got them expedited."

"That's great! What happened to the punk who shot me?"

"You mean after Nikki drained her stunner in him? He had nearly as many bounties as his folks."

"How long have I been out?"

"Two days. It's Thursday morning. We went ahead and did the full package while we had you inside anyway. Nikki said you'd just find excuses not to if we waited."

"Always something to do around here. I need to get back to Dingus' ride."

"Nope. Dee and Dingus finished getting it ready to fly. Dingus hauled off the plague saucer to the Patrol base. I sent in Dee's pictures. I figure her new ID should be here anytime. You have a message to call the lawyer when you can. Anything else you feel a need to be worrying about at this particular moment in time?"

"I gotta whiz."

Max spoke up, "That's our Bob, always practical."

I raised my head and looked around. The basement was full. Dee, Dingus, Lyla and Max were there, but also our paintball team, Julie, Jacob, NotherBob, Jason, and Jack, who was in uniform. "Is it Sunday already?", I asked.

Julie said, "Very funny, Bob, we're not here for paintball. You scared the crap out of all of us."

"You're right. All that good training, and as soon as a kid sounds pathetic, I'm a newbie all over again. Pure stupid. Wish this machine could cure that."

John said, "A man has got to know his limitations."

"All right Clint, find me some pants."

Everyone but John and Nikki adjourned upstairs, to avoid seeing things they'd rather not. When I sat up, I realized I had a nasty headache. "I hope there's coffee. I have entirely too much blood in my caffeine system."

Nikki said, "Let's get you upstairs, Caveman."

When I had taken care of what I needed to do, I went in the kitchen where everyone was congregated. There was an enormous amount of food. After we had all eaten, and everyone was reassured that, indeed, Bob was okay, people began leaving. It struck me that I never realized how much my friends cared about me. After the paintball team was gone, Lyla said to Nikki, "Can you run me over to my saucer? I need to get back and file my story."

Nikki replied, "Let me get the key to the barn, and I'll be right there."

Dingus came and sat by me. He said, "Bob, I know you've been awfully busy lately, but you REALLY need to take the tactical training courses. All the way up to the advanced special that I wrote."

"Understood, sir."

"You don't have to be all official about it, Bob. We all make mistakes. I just don't want to deal with Nikki if you mess up and get yourself killed."

"Oh, self preservation, now I understand. I wanted to ask you, but I never got the chance. Is there any way to become a Guide auxiliary base or something, so we have supplies for these kinds of things on hand?"

"I'll see what I can do when I'm back there. I'm sure things have changed in the last hundred years, so I couldn't say for sure, but we should be able to get a medkit, with all the essentials. No cure for dumbass, though."

"I deserve that. Are you coming back after you file paperwork?"

"I don't think Dee wants to leave permanently, but we may do a little sightseeing while we're gone. You need us back for something?"

"Dee's cooking, mostly."

Dee spoke up, "Listen at that line of crap. You know you need my man here to bail you out when your bulldog mouth overloads your canary ass!"

Dingus said, "She does have a point."

I replied, "She does, at that."

When Nikki got back, she said, "Bob, that robot you left at the other place got bored. You hadn't shut it down all the way. It organized the barn. Even you can find things now."

"Oops. Did you shut it off?"

"Yes, Caveman, I can remember to take care of things."

Dingus spoke up, "I think she can keep you on the straight and narrow for a few weeks. We're going to take off." He hugged Nikki, shook hands with the rest of us. Dee had hugs for everyone. "You take care of one another, you hear?"

Nikki and I drove them to the other place to get their ride. Dingus said, "I hope you don't mind, I grabbed some parts off the salvage."

"I don't mind. Just curious, what did you get?"

"Dee wanted bigger drive emitters, since we have the power to run them, and I found a better flight computer. How it wound up in that piece of junk is a mystery. Few other bits and pieces, nothing major."

"At least Dee's got a hot rod. Teach her to fly and she'll be happy."

Dee said, "He did that while you were snoozing, Caveman."

Nikki was right, the barn did look a lot easier to find things in. We said our last goodbyes, and the happy couple headed for the stars. Nikki asked, "We going back to John's?"

"There's nothing here, not even a sleeping bag to put down, and we're out of food in town. It's probably best for now. Besides, it's what Snitz is used to."

Just then I realized, Snitz had laid by my feet the whole time Dingus had taken off. I got out my communicator and called him. "Hey Dingus, could you do me a favor?"

"Sure, Bob, what do you need?"

"Can you make another pass over us, say 10,000 feet, not too fast?"

"Okay? What's up, Bob?"

"Snitz slept through you taking off."

"Oh, I see. Let's find out. There, did he wake up?"

"Nope. That was easy. We'll have to see how the damping I put in holds up. See you later."

"Bye Bob."

Near John's, we met a car we didn't recognize coming from his place. When we got in, I asked, "Who was that?"

John said, "Dee's papers. She won't need them 'til she gets back, anyhow."

"Seems so quiet, all of a sudden."

"Won't stay that way, will it?"

"Probably not."

Nikki and I decided to stay in the saucer again. We said our goodnights and took Snitz to bed.

Miraculously, I woke up before Snitz. We checked to see which plants needed watered and fertilized, and then we wandered up to the house. John had coffee going. I asked, "When does the lawyer make it to the office? Nine o'clock?"

"I would think so. What do you have him working on, anyway?"

"Finding Dee's Chevelle. I hope he's not going to tell me it got crushed."

"What are you doing with that?"

"Fix it up for her, let her teach the kids some manners."

"What else you got going?"

"I'm thinking I need a better workshop than that barn we're storing stuff in, and that workshop that came with the place isn't big enough for what we need to do. I need to see about a metal building, and a slab to put it on."

"With the kind of money we've got, that shouldn't be a problem."

"Yes and no. I don't want a crew hanging around over there getting into things."

"You two going to move in over there?"

"That's on my list as well. You see anything I'm missing?"

"Training, like Dingus said."

"After breakfast."

I made omelets, and Nikki was up and around by the time they were ready. Max came dragging in about then, too. When the dishes were taken care of, I went with John to start training. By the time I was alert again, it was time to call the lawyer. I got his secretary, who told me the car had been found, sitting in a backyard with a blown engine. She gave me the address of the place. I thanked her, and said goodbye. I asked, "Anybody want to help move?" A chorus of "Sure, why not." was my answer. We took Nikki's rig, and she dropped me at the rental place. I got the biggest truck they had, since money wasn't a problem, and fewer trips would be less hassle. Lots of boxes, a couple of dollies, and I was ready to go. With all of us working, well, Snitz was supervising, it went fairly quickly. We pretty much got the house the first load, and after we got it into the new place, we went to lunch. The next load was the rest of the house and the portable stuff from the shop. By the time that was unloaded, we were hungry again. We returned the truck, and went out to eat. Julie traded tables to serve us, and asked, "So what are you guys up to?"

Nikki said, "Moving Caveman's stuff out to our farm."

"So you guys are setting up house?"

"Still have some unpacking to do, but yeah, we are."

"A courier brought me some odd papers today, said a distant cousin had died and left me some money."

I said, "They got that processed? Good deal!"

"Where did that come from?"

"Bounties on those folks you helped catch the other day."

"I don't have any idea what to do with that kind of money."

"Let it sit until you need it, then. It won't rot."

"So you guys got a cut too?"

"Not from this batch, we got the money for the base."

"But you were there for this one too, why not take it?"

"We already have more than we know what to do with."

When we finished, we rolled by the Chevelle. It was in bad shape, with a few dents, lots of rust, and up on blocks. I went to the door and knocked. "Hi, I'm Bob Wilson. I was wondering if you would consider selling that Chevelle in the back yard?"

"That's a classic, a '68. It's a factory 427 car, rare as can be."

I knew that was BS, Dee had told me about scrounging motor mounts from an SS396, and putting in the 427 from an Impala, but I let him run. "So what do you figure it's worth?"

"At least a hundred grand. Be worth a lot more when I get it fixed up." I got a funny vibe off the guy, he kept looking beside the door where a shotgun would lean. I decided not to press the issue. "I see. Sorry to bother you, I was just looking for a project car myself, didn't realize it was something special."

I backed off the porch, and kept an eye on him 'til I got back to Nikki's truck. I climbed in and said, "Drive."

John asked, "So, no luck?"

"He was deciding whether or not to pull a shotgun on me just for asking about it. I didn't think getting Dee the exact same VIN was worth a gunfight."

Nikki asked, "What's a VIN?"

"Vehicle identification number. It proves which vehicle belongs to which paperwork."

"Like a transponder code."

"Exactly, except these are little metal tags scattered around the car."

"Scattered, how do you mean?"

"They're attached in different places, to try and make sure no one with bad intent knows where they all are."

John asked, "Why do you think he was so hinky about you asking his price?"

"I dunno, but hopefully, it's not our problem."

We stopped so Nikki and I could get some groceries for the farm. We went by and dropped them off, and took John home. Max was going to stay there for the time being. I took the next tactical course. I was really beginning to feel stupid for having rushed in and gotten shot. We loaded up Snitz, and headed home. When we got there, I walked around the truck and caught Nikki before she started unloading. "Caveman, what are you doing? We need to get this stuff in the house!"

"Ancient caveman custom. Just take a minute." I picked her up to carry her in the house. Luckily, she had her keys handy, so I didn't have to fumble for mine while carrying her. Once inside, I set her down and kissed her.

"What was that all about?"

"It's called 'carrying her over the threshold' and it's supposed to bring good fortune to a newly married couple."

"So we can bring in groceries now?"

"Yes."

"Do I get a ride back, too?"

"Sure, why not."

It took a while to figure out where to store everything. Snitz took a few minutes to find all the smells in the house. We sat in front of the TV, and I realized I hadn't had any service turned on. We watched a movie, and ate popcorn, and snuggled. At least, we tried. Apparently, a dog's place is in the middle.

I guess moving a bed makes it new again. Anyway it seemed to need a lot of breaking in. Entirely too early, it was time to make sure that this new house had an outdoors, too. Snitz found many new things to smell. He was very interested in the cellar, where Dingus had been in suspension. I suppose hundred year old jerky is like fine wine, to a dog. By the time we had everything checked out, Nikki had coffee started, and was working on breakfast.

"So what do you have planned today, Caveman?"

"We need TV and internet for the house, I need to check into getting a slab poured for a new shop, and I should start looking for a different car to fix up for Dee."

"Do you think she'll mind not having the same car?"

"With that idiot just letting it rust in his backyard? I'd be shocked if she wasn't. It would cause more trouble than we can afford to force the issue, though."

When we were through with the dishes, I got out my phone and got to work. When I started looking at buildings and slabs, I realized I had no idea where I wanted to put it. Obviously, Snitz would need to help me find the right spot. "Hey, Space Cadet, we're going for a walk. You want to come along?"

"Sounds good. When are the installation guys supposed to get here?"

"They both said they could make it this afternoon. Should we take the Frisbee?"

"Let's. This is sounding better all the time."

We found a low spot not too far from the house that would keep the shop from being easy to see from the road. I stepped it off, and it was plenty big enough for the building I had looked at. I found some fair sized sticks, and roughed in where I wanted the corners. Work done, it was Frisbee time. Other than a few bad landings, Snitz was really getting the hang of it. I wish I had video of the time he snowballed all the way down the hill with the Frisbee in his teeth. Youtube would love that. Snitz got tired, we got hungry, and it was time to get some lunch.

While we were eating, I had an idea. "Space Cadet, can mechanic bots be programmed for other tasks?"

"Like what, Caveman?"

"Excavation, or carpentry, for example."

"That sounds easy enough. I was afraid you wanted a haircut."

"Not today. I was thinking about letting them do the forms for the slab."

I took out a pencil and paper and calculated the amount of lumber required. I added some, for Murphy, and put in an order with the lumber yard. They could deliver that afternoon. I showed Nikki what the bots needed to do, and she set them up. We spent the afternoon dealing with installers and deliveries. When that was done, I asked, "We have that nice big barbecue pit out back. You think we should try it out and invite John and Max over to eat supper?"

"Roasted animal parts? My favorite! Let's do that."

I called John, and he said they would be over about supper time. Now that I had internet with a decent sized screen, I started looking for a car for Dee. I found some already fixed up, but nothing I thought she would really like. I found lots of rust buckets, buy a title and build a car from scratch sort of things. However, finding something solid enough to build without a full restoration, was quite a hunt. Nikki told me it was time to start the fire before I found one I liked.

John and Max showed up, and we sat and talked while supper cooked. Max wanted to see the cellar where his dad had been in suspension. John said he would watch supper while I showed it to him. I got a light and the key, and we went down to Dingus' chamber. He looked at the equipment stored for Dingus' awakening, marveling at how crude it was compared to what he was used to. Then he looked at the readouts on the power core, and got a shocked look on his face. "It was a closer call than I thought. He wouldn't have had power for much longer."

"We've had a run of good luck."

We went up to eat. I mentioned to John the trouble I was having finding a decent car for Dee. He said, "Can't you buy nearly all the parts as reproductions? Why not just buy one of those titles with rust attached? At least that way, you know she has a solid car."

"You're probably right. It would be easier to build one from scratch than try to fix everything wrong with an old one. I was just trying to be a hard head."

"Stick with what you're good at, I guess."

"Thanks, John. It's so good to have your support."

"Anytime. All part of the service. When do you plan to start this great project?"

"I had thought to wait until the new shop was up, but that's going to be a couple of weeks. I don't want to tie up your garage, in case we get customers, so I'm not sure what to do."

"Doesn't this place have a garage?"

"Duh. I haven't even been in there. I wonder what it's like?"

That prompted an expedition to check it out. It wasn't big enough to park a saucer in, but it might work. The shelves held all sorts of interesting old bits and pieces. Looked like nobody had bothered to clean it out in a long time. "This might do, after it's cleaned up."

John said, "At least it's a place to get started, until your new shop is ready."

"I think I'll see if I can get one those bored bots in here to clean it up."

It was getting dark. I said, "Nikki and I have a little project going tonight, you guys wanna see?"

John replied, "Not sure about that, Bob. Are there whips and chains involved?"

"Bots and shovels and hammers, no whips, no chains."

"Bots and shovels and hammers, Oh My!"

"Come on, Dorothy."

We got the bots out of the barn and led them down to where we were putting the new shop. Nikki set up her program, and they started digging. It was amazing how far they could throw a shovelful of dirt. I asked Nikki, "They do know to get back under cover before daylight, don't they?"

"I put that in the program, but they will probably be done before then anyhow."

"Forms and all?"

"Yep. Do you want me to have one of them work in the garage tomorrow?"

"That would be wonderful. It's not too much trouble?'

"No trouble at all. Cleaning a work area is one of their standard duties."

"Don't they have to charge?", John asked.

"They have tiny little power cores. No, Bob, they won't show on a scanner."

"But they don't bother Snitz."

Snitz, hearing his name, thought surely that treats or Frisbee were about to happen.

Nikki said, "They don't, do they." She fiddled with her watch and said, "How about that. Since the cores are smaller, they rattle at a much higher frequency, one that even Snitz can't hear."

Max said, "Who would have thought an Earther hillbilly could teach us about power cores?"

"Hillbilly, huh? Max has been into the culture pack, methinks.", I said.

John replied, "So it would seem."

Satisfied Nikki had the bots well programmed, we went back to the house. John and Max said their goodnights and headed back to John's. We decided to make an early evening of it, since we hadn't been sleeping much. About two in the morning, I was awakened by what sounded like gunfire. I grabbed my jeans, my rifle, and a flashlight, and went to see what was going on. The sound was coming from the work site. As I got closer, I saw just what a bot with a claw hammer can do. Sinking framing nails with one blow makes a lot of noise. Three bots doing it together at ridiculous rates is really noisy. If the sound was carrying, we could easily have concerned neighbors calling the Sheriff. I called John. "Wha? Why you calling, Bob? Snitz hear something?"

"So you don't hear the bots doing carpentry?"

"What? No, I don't hear any hammering. Are YOU hammered?"

"Just wanted to make sure we weren't going to have neighbors calling the Sheriff. I didn't want to have to explain why I have alien robots building concrete forms in the middle of the night."

"Let me step out on the porch and be sure, but my house is closer than any of the others. If I can't hear it, chances are nobody else can."

"Okay, thanks."

"Bob, I can hear a distant rumble, but it doesn't sound all that odd. I think you're okay. I'm going back to bed."

"Night, John."

Soon enough, the bots finished up. They gathered their tools and went back to the barn. Then the one started for the garage, and I ran ahead to put the door up.

The bot started in, I put the door down and went back to bed. Snitz got up early, I think it was revenge for leaving him inside when I got up. We went outside to take care of business, and when we got back, I started some coffee. I decided to check the garage while the coffee was brewing. The bot had cleaned the place up, and straightened all the clutter on the shelves. I was surprised when it reported to me in English. "Sir, these bags contain items that appear to be of no further value. I will send an inventory of them to your communicator if you wish to check my work. The shelves have been organized according to what my programming deemed to be a logical scheme. If you wish them organized differently, please tell me what scheme to use. This box contains items that I can repair. This other box contains items which I do not recognize. Is my work satisfactory?"

"Yes, quite satisfactory. Do you have a name?"

"Name, sir?"

"A designation more specific than just 'robot'?"

"I am number ZZ809 of my model, sir."

"ZZ809, you say. Would it be acceptable if I referred to you as 'Topper'?"
"Of course, sir, as you wish."
"It will require you having an identifying mark to distinguish you from the other units. Is that acceptable?"
"Yes, sir."
I saw some trim paint, masking tape, and a brush on the shelf. Where Topper had found those in this mess was beyond me. After some consideration, I decided he could probably paint a better logo than I could. I showed him a ZZ Top logo on my phone, and asked him to paint the design on his chest plate, with the name Topper underneath. I watched, fascinated as he painted, and then used a built in heat gun to quick dry the paint.
"Nice work, Topper. After you clean your brush, you may shut down. I will have more for you to do later."
"Very good, sir."
I returned to the kitchen to find Nikki already up, with a cup of coffee.
"Where you been, Caveman?"
"Out in the garage, talking to Topper."
"Topper? Oh, you named the bot."
"After breakfast, you want to wander down with me and check out the forms they made last night?"
"Sounds good. What else do we need to do today?"
"I was going to get some of the maintenance bots started on those saucers we brought home, see if we can get them in good shape, instead of just flyable. I need to see about getting the slab poured for the new shop, maybe see about getting power run back there, and find a car for Dee."
"Sounds like a busy day. No time for Space Cadets?"
"Always time for Space Cadets. If it doesn't all get done today, it's not a biggie. It's just that things have a way of popping up around here, and making things get put off."
After we ate, Snitz led us down to the shop. He thought it would be another Frisbee morning. It was beautifully done. I looked at Nikki and said, "Your program worked very well."
"Thanks."
"Wish they could pour the concrete, too."
"Why couldn't they?"

"This slab will take several truck loads of concrete. I don't think they can mix fast enough to fill the forms before it begins to set. That would make weak spots."

"Let me check some things before you hire a crew, okay?"

"Sure."

We went back by the barn, and Nikki helped me get things rolling on fixing up those saucers. Back at the house, Nikki studied concrete construction, while I made phone calls. I got on the internet, and found a donor car not too far away at a reasonable price. When I called, the lady said she would be there all afternoon, and I should come prepared to load it myself.

"Space Cadet, you want to go for a ride?"

"I sure do. Come this way, Caveman."

Sometime later, we got organized to go out. We went to the bank and got some cash, and the U-Haul place for a car trailer and a big enough truck to pull it. I threw some tools in the back of the truck, and we left mine at the rental place. Mrs. Tucker was very nice, sold us the car no problem. I was glad I had brought the compressor, it had three flats. We got it loaded, and started back. Nikki asked, "You hungry, Caveman?"

"I am. See anyplace you like?"

"I don't know. What's barbecue?"

"Roasted animal parts. With sauce."

"Let's do that."

We pulled in, and I took Snitz to take care of business. I put him in truck, and we went in. "Hey, folks, sit anywhere, I'll be right with you."

We sat down, and she brought us menus. "My name's Barb, and I'm your server today. Can I get you something to drink?"

Nikki said, "Coke, please."

I said, "I'll take an unsweet tea."

"Be right back."

Nikki said, "So many choices. I don't know what I want."

"Get a sampler, then. See, it's right there.", I pointed.

"That works. What are you getting?"

"This deal with burnt ends and sausage sounds good to me."

Barb came back with the drinks and saw our menus on the table. "Ready to order, then?"

"Yes, Ma'am."

We told her what we wanted, and she turned in the order. When our lunch came, it was very good. We left a nice tip, and got back on the road. Topper's brothers helped me get the car in the barn when we got to the farm, and we took the rental back. Nikki looked at a mixer they had for rent. "One cubic yard, hmm, how many cubic yards do you need for the slab?"

"Eighty, probably. Need to order a hundred just to be sure."

"How long does this machine take to mix?"

"Fifteen or twenty minutes, I'd guess. Too long, anyway. The first part of the pour would be setting up before we got all of it poured."

All the way home, she was messing with her watch, I could tell she was trying to figure something out.

"Caveman, Not very many Earth people are ever going to be in your shop, right?"

"Other than certified people? I wouldn't think so. I was hoping to have a workspace where I wouldn't have to keep saucer parts hidden."

"So you were doing concrete just because that's the way it's done here?"

"I suppose so, yes. You have a better option?"

"We have a construction material similar to what you folks call epoxy granite. The pirates had a bunch of it, and a machine to put it in with, that they used to build their base."

"You're telling me we've got the materials and tools to put the slab in ourselves?"

"You probably want a maintenance bot to go over the pouring machine before we start, but I think we do."

"Space Cadet, what would I do without you?"

"Get too drunk to fish?"

"John mentioned that, did he?"

"John? Who is this John of whom you speak?"

"Slick, Space Cadet, real slick."

When we got back to our place, I went over the inventory and found the machine Nikki had talked about. I put a bot on it, and went to do more internet research. Looking into reproduction parts, I found it was pretty much possible to build a car from scratch, now that I had a clear title to attach to it. I figured the bots could put it together straighter and stronger than anything that ever came out of Detroit. By the time I finished ordering pieces, my bank card said ouch, but I had a good start on a car for Dee.

My phone rang. "Hi John, what's up?"

"Why don't you guys come over for supper? You have training to do yet anyway, don't you?"

"Sounds good. We'll be over in a little bit."

I found Nikki working with her watch. Since she got it hooked into the house wireless, she had been learning about Earth from the internet.
"Whatcha learnin', Space Cadet?"
"I found some old pictures on the Historical Society website. I think they might help you."
"Help me how?"
She put up the holographic display, and I could see photos of a car show from a few years back. One of the featured cars was Dee's Chevelle, in its prime. "Does this show you what you'll need to know to get it like it was?"
"It will help a lot. Do you think you can program the bots to do that paint job?"
"You want to get tickled, is that it?"
"So sorry, your magnificence, I did not mean to cast asparagus on your skills."
"The Stooges, you went with the Stooges?"
I did the only thing I could think of in the moment. I bunched my eyebrows, mimed a cigar, and said, "That's the most ridiculous thing I've ever heard."
"Groucho, now! We're gonna be late for supper if you keep this crap up."
We got ready and Nikki drove us to John's. Snitz was glad to see Max, and I think the feeling was mutual. We had a wonderful supper. Who knew Max could cook? "John, you were right about starting from scratch on Dee's car. I picked up a title with rust attached, and ordered some parts. Hope she doesn't mind I'm going a little more modern on some things."
"Like what?"
"LS instead of a big block, six speeds instead of four, suspension that actually handles."
"I don't know about that last. She do love her sideways."
"It'll have enough power to get sideways, even with the good suspension."
"What about looks?"
"Nikki found pictures of an old car show she was in. That should give us a good idea. If we have to, we can always send a drone over to scan the real thing."
"That would be a little risky, don't you think?"
"Yep. I'd rather manage without. It was a pretty nice car. I have to wonder if it was ever in a magazine?"
Nikki fiddled with her watch. "Found it in Car Craft. Nice catch, Caveman!"
My communicator gave a small chime. Nikki said, "That your girlfriend texting you, Caveman?"

"Nope. She uses a cell phone."

"Asshole!"

After the tickle fight, I looked at the message. The epoxy granite machine was ready to rock. I said to John, "I better get to that training, looks like I need to be back by dark."

"Hot date?"

"Probably, but we need to get the bots started on the slab."

"The bots can do concrete?"

"Nikki found a load of one of their construction materials in the stuff we brought home. Works at least as good, and we have the machine to put it in with."

"Won't that look odd?'

"It's what the pirate base was made out of. Didn't look that much different than regular concrete, did you think?"

"Not really, no. You got lucky on that one."

"She's a wonder."

"I meant the concrete."

"That too."

John set me up to train. When I woke up, I was even more aggravated at myself for letting that punk get the drop on me. "How many more of these do I have to do?"

"Two more regular ones, and then Dingus' special. Why?"

"Well, John, I'm getting tired of waking up pissed at myself for getting shot."

"Now you know how we felt, Bob."

"Sympathy. It's a wonderful thing."

It was just getting good dark when we got home. I got Topper out of the garage, and he showed me all the items from his repair box, good as new. I told him I was very pleased with his work, and we went down to the barn to get the other bots. "Unit ZZ809, you have contamination on your chest plate. Do you require aid to remove it?"

"Unit OZ753, it is not contamination. It is the designation of this unit. I am now known as Topper."

"We are to be given new designations? What is mine to be?"

I asked, "What is your current designation?"

"OZ753. Sir."

"Ozzie it is." I found a cartoon of Ozzie biting a bat, and told Topper, "At your earliest convenience, can you put this logo, and the name O-z-z-i-e, on OZ753?'

"Of course, sir."

The third cargo bot approached. "Am I to have a new designation as well. Sir?"

"If you desire one, of course."

"I do."

"What is your current designation?"

"TZ115, sir."

"And you shall be Taz." I looked up the appropriate cartoon, and sent it to Topper.

"But right now, we have work to do."

We got the epoxy machine headed to the shop site, and the boys started carrying the raw material to feed it. Soon, the slab was going in at an amazing rate. I told Topper to text me when they finished, or to retreat to the barn if they weren't done by sunup, and went back to the house. Snitz dealt with his business on the way, we were able to hit the rack when we got back. About three thirty, I got the text from Topper. I went and let him into the garage, so he could ink up his brothers. When they finished, I followed them to the garage, and locked up behind them.

I crawled back into bed, and Nikki mumbled, "Get it, done, Caveman?"

"All good, Space Cadet."

Snitz decided it was perimeter check time early, even though he had gone out with me during the night.

We wandered down and looked at the slab. It looked like it would pass for concrete, and it was already set up. Gotta love high tech construction! Back at the house, I started coffee, and sat down to look at the magazine article Nikki had found. It had enough detail to fill in some of the blanks about how Dee had set the car up. It was beginning to sound like I might be on the right track with the changes I was making. If I could just get it put together before they got back.

Nikki came into the kitchen, and I poured her a cup. "They do a good job on the slab, Caveman?"

"Looks great. I'm going to order the building kit today, and see about getting power run out there. By the way, all the cargo bots have names now. Topper, Ozzie, and Taz."

She looked something up on her watch. "OZ753, that would be Ozzie, TZ115, Taz, that makes sense, how do you get from ZZ809 to Topper?"

"ZZ Top, the band."

More fiddling. "Okay, I see now."

After we ate, I made a couple of phone calls, and ordered a few more parts online. I found Nikki just finishing an episode of Woodwright's Shop. "I'm glad you showed me this, Caveman, it's fascinating how he gets such good results with the old tools. He's funny, too."

"Glad you like it. I'm going to run to town and get a few things dealt with, you want to ride along?"

"I want a shower first."

"Need help?"

It was sometime later before we made it to town. We got the title transferred on the Chevelle, turned in our marriage license, and got my mail changed to the farm. We went by and emptied the old mailbox, and checked on the old place. Snitz found some scents there he was very interested in, and found he needed to respond to some pee mail. It was getting close to lunch time, so we went by to see Julie, and get something to eat. She met us at the door and asked, "Your usual drinks?"

We said, "Sounds good." and found a place to sit. When Julie came to get our orders, she said, "Things are a little up in the air today. The owner mentioned he was thinking of retiring, and everyone's a little worried about what's going to happen."

I looked at her and said, "Really? You know this place inside and out. We both know the money isn't a problem, so make him an offer and settle the place down."

"But what if I can't make a go of it?"

"You have enough spendolium to keep the doors open 'til you figure it out, don't you?"

"Curse you, Red Baron!"

"I want to fly like a beagle, to the sea. Fly like a beagle, let my Sopwith carry me."

Nikki said, "Ouch. Julie, you're almost as bad as John. Look what you made him do."

"Nikki, you say the nicest things."

Julie brought our lunch, still half glaring at me for pointing out the obvious to her. We left a nice tip, and headed home. The crew from the electric company nearly beat us there. I showed them where we needed the power, and got out of their way. Snitz was concerned about so many strangers in his yard, so I took him down towards the pond and tired him out with the Frisbee. When we got back, the crew had made good progress, and it looked like they could finish today. About the time I got sat down with a glass of tea, the trucks with the building kit showed up. I showed them where it needed to go, and they unloaded. I brought in the instruction book, and gave it to Nikki. "Oh, for me, how nice Caveman! What's next, a pretty apron and matching spatulas?"

"If I try to program it, it'll come out looking like it was designed by Frank Lloyd Wrong."

"So you're saying my Kung Fu is best?"

"I gotta find more for you to do, TV is gonna rot your brain."

"You have met my dog, Payback?"

"Yeah, she have her pups yet?"

By the time the power crew was ready to leave, it was getting to be supper time. I asked if Nikki would like to go out, and she said yes. I called John, and he said they were interested as well. We went over to John's, and I took another training course. Then we went out. Julie met us at the door, "Oh, it's my favorite shit stirrer. How are you all tonight?"

John said, "Doing well, what did Bob do this time?"

"Talked me into buying this place."

"Good for you! How many times have you said you wanted to?"

"Not you too, John?"

"Just the facts, ma'am."

"Find a table, Joe."

A couple of the other servers and the cook made a point of coming by and thanking me for talking to Julie. I didn't think I had that kind of influence, but they seemed to think I had saved their jobs. Dee better not hear about this one, or she'd buy me a cape for sure. On the way home, John asked, "So what's next, Kemosabe?"

"Nikki's got Topper and the boys putting up the shop tonight. I'll get them some wire and pipe tomorrow, so they can get the electrical and plumbing set up. Hope to move my heavy stuff tomorrow night."

"Who's Topper?"

Nikki said, "Bob's named the cargo bots. Ozzie, Topper, and Taz. They're psyched about it, got emblems painted on their chest plates."

John asked, "I know I will regret this, but how did he come up with those names?"

"He used the prefixes of their serial numbers. Ozzie is OZ753, Taz is TZ115, and Topper is ZZ809."

"ZZ Top, Bob?"

"I'm just lookin' for some tush."

"I think you've already found more than you can handle."

"You could be right, John."

It was getting dark by the time we got back, and John wanted to see the bots' ink, so we went by our place to get them started. John looked at their art, and said, "Did you do these, Bob? This is good work."

"No. Topper there did those, even his own."

Nikki downloaded what they needed to do. I got the feeling she had improved some of the procedure, but I knew whatever she was up to, it would come out cool.

After she finished, she ran John and Max back. I sat and watched the bots for a while, still amazed at how skilled they were. Snitz and I went back to the house when we heard Nikki pull in. "Caveman, where are you? Come quick!"

We ran the rest of the way to the house. "What's the matter, Space Cadet?"

"Jack brought in a casualty while I was over at John's. His saucer crashed, and you need to take the freighter and get it under cover."

"I'll get the boys. Take Snitz."

I jumped in the truck, and drove down to the new shop. "Down tools, boys, we've got an emergency."

They stopped what they were doing and climbed aboard. I tarped them and drove for John's.

When we got there, Max handed me directions Jack had written out. I opened the barn, and got the boys on the freighter. I parked and idled as close as I could get to the wreck. The boys jumped out and brought it aboard, and we were airborne again. I took it to our place, since we would soon have a shop to work on it in. After they unloaded the saucer, Topper asked, "Should we resume our other duties, sir?"

"Yes, please. You boys did good. Thank you."

"Sir, you treat us differently than our other owners have. It is very kind of you."

"You work hard. You deserve respect. Nothing special."

"It is to us, sir."

I got some of the smaller bots checking over the wreck, then I took the freighter back to John's. After I closed up the barn, I went to the house to find out what was happening. John met me at the door. "Did you get the saucer under cover, Bob?"

"It's in my barn getting checked over. Will that do?"

"I think so. We need to call the Patrol."

"Why?"

"It's Bill. I've got him in the autodoc, but it'll be a while before I can get him out. His uncle needs to know, Bob."

"You're right, as much as I hate to make the call, it's got to be done."

I got out my communicator and dialed the Patrol. "Patrol Headquarters, how may I direct your call?"

"Could I speak with Major Rottum, please?"

"Who may I say is calling?"

"Bob Wilson, acceptable contact. Please tell him it's regarding his nephew, Bill."

"One moment, please."

"Mr. Wilson, what is it now?"

"Major, your nephew has crashed a saucer here. We have him in the autodoc, and we've recovered the wreckage."

"How badly injured is he?"

"One moment, sir, I'll put you on with our medic."

I handed the comm to John. "Major, the autodoc has him stabilized, with a treatment estimate of two days, local."

John handed me the comm. "Yes, Major?"

"How did this happen, Mr. Wilson?"

"Sir, I don't know. One of our crew was first on the scene, and brought Bill in for medical attention. I went out and recovered the craft. Until someone reviews the logs, I doubt we'll have much idea exactly what happened."

"So your crew just happened to find the wreck before anyone else?"

"He's law enforcement. He was called to what was thought to be an airplane crash."

"You say he should be up and around in two days?"

"Yes, sir. We'll call you as soon as he's awake."

"Very good, Mr. Wilson."

He disconnected. "Well, John that wasn't quite as bad as I expected. Wonder what he has up his sleeve?"

"I'd have Nikki check Bill's ride for trackers, first."

"You think he'd sic pirates on us?"

"You think he wouldn't?"

"Gotta go."

I called Nikki and asked her to start checking for trackers, and make a certified copy of the log from that saucer. When I got back, Nikki was in the barn, working. I went down to see what she had found. "I found two, Caveman. We don't have a stash box like John, so I had to destroy them, but I got good images first. This thing is even worse than that heap he had me flying. I don't know how he got it in the air, much less this far."

"Did you get the log?"

"Certified copy, just like you wanted. You think the major is going to try and railroad us?"

"Couldn't bet against it. Wish Dingus was here."

"At least the Guide got his ID certified while they were here. Pity some Caveman was dumb enough to get shot, I wanted to introduce you to some people."

"That is a shame. Maybe we'll go see them sometime."

I looked at the report on the saucer. Nikki was right, the surprise wasn't that it had crashed, but that it got as far as it did. All of its inspections were current, though. Looked like someone was selling phony inspections.

Having done what I could for now, I walked down to see how the boys were getting along on the shop. Snitz was afraid I might get lost in the dark, and volunteered to be my guide. The fellas were down to hanging the doors. I've never seen a roll up door go up that slick. Topper asked, "Sir, we have completed our task. Should we return to the barn?"

"No, Topper, why don't you guys stay here. I'll bring you some more supplies and instructions tomorrow. You fellas really do nice work."

"Thank you, sir."

Snitz and I went back to the barn. Nikki looked as if she had finished what she was doing. "Caveman, do you think we should let the bots start fixing this junk heap?"

"Leave it. Don't want to be accused of tampering with evidence."

"I'm finished, then."

"Do you think you can tell the fellas how to wire and plumb the shop tomorrow? I promised them more work."

"You and those bots. You'd think they were your kids or something."

"Speaking of which, we gotta practice, don't we?"

"Slow learner that you are, it may take years to teach you anything."

Regardless of how late we were up, Snitz took his duty as an alarm clock seriously. I started coffee on the way out, so it would be ready when I got back. The new shop looked even better in the daylight. It struck me that those bots weren't actually on the planet legally. I had a crew of illegal aliens doing construction work on my place in the dark of night. Somehow, an ICE raid wasn't high on my list of worries.

Even coffee wasn't powerful enough to rouse Nikki that day. I decided to make a list of everything we needed to finish off the new shop while I was waiting to have breakfast with her. It looked like I could get it all in my truck, but it would be more loaded than it had been in a long time. Finally Snitz got tired of waiting, and got Nikki up. I made breakfast while she was communing with the coffee gods. "I've got to run in and get that stuff for the boys, I doubt you would have a place to sit on the way back."

"You sure it's not that you're tired of me already?"

It took me a while to prove that wasn't true.

I got everything on my list at the lumberyard, and I got it all in the truck, but there were a couple of fellas watching to see how I was going to get it all loaded. I think I got extra points when I pulled a red bandana out of the glove box, and flagged the pipe hanging out the back. When I made it back, Nikki was sitting on the porch petting Snitz. "Hey good lookin', bring the Frisbee, and we'll have some fun."

She went in and got the disc, and they followed me down to the shop. Nikki had shown me how to call the bots on the comm, so I called and asked Topper to raise the door. I backed in, and asked, "Can you boys help me unload?"

"Yes, sir."

With the boys help, it didn't take long to get unloaded and the materials stacked out of the way. I had a thought. I got the disc from Nikki, and threw it at Topper. It took a half second for him to perceive what was happening, and then he caught it. "Sir, I believe you misplaced this."

"No, I meant to throw it to you. Throw it back, please."

Topper trying to throw a Frisbee overhand was too comical for words. I demonstrated the technique. He froze for a second, I assume calculating trajectories. He said, "You mean like this, sir?", as he sailed it to Nikki.

"Exactly. Can you teach your brothers?"

"I can, sir."

Shortly, we had a five way game of Frisbee going, with Snitz only occasionally catching the disc. He had fun chasing it, though. Once Snitz got tired, Nikki helped me explain how I wanted the shop wired and plumbed. The need for two systems of plumbing, water, and compressed air was a stumbling point, but soon they understood the whole plan. Topper showed me a hologram of their understanding, and it looked right. Nikki and I left them to it, and took Snitz back to the house. Nikki said, "I've never seen cargo bots used for recreational purposes before."

"Recreational purposes? No, serious business. Exercising an important saucer detecting animal, definitely mission critical work, don't you think?"

"Dee's right, you must wear blue contacts."

We were heading into the house when my phone rang. It was the trucker with the first shipment of Chevelle parts, confirming we would be home to receive them. I told him we would be around all day, and he asked for directions. Seems G.P. Guess didn't know where we lived. I got him squared away. When I sat down with a cup of coffee, the comm chimed. It was Sargent Darning. "Good morning, Sargent, what can I do for you today?"

"Bob, the Major would like you to haul his nephew's saucer here."

"Not a problem. How soon would he like it?"

"I believe he said, 'Right frikkin' now'."

"He is aware daylight operations increase our chance of discovery?"

"That didn't seem to concern him."

"I see. I'll get it loaded and underway this morning, then."

"Nikki, sweetheart, could you do me a favor?"

"Caveman, you want something, don't you?"

"Well, yes I do, but that will have to wait. Major Rottum wants Bill's saucer, and I quote, 'right frikkin' now'."

"What does that have to do with me, Caveman?"

"If me and the boys load it, could you fly it out to him?"

"What's in it for me?"

"Roasted animal parts?"

"I think I may need to go shopping. Do you think Julie would have time?"

"Could it wait 'til you get back?"

"If I put it off, I might need more things."

"Whatever it takes."

She went and got the freighter, while I left Snitz in the house and went to get the boys. I had them carry the tarp over their heads as we walked to the barn. If anyone ever examined satellite photos we were in a world of hurt, but there was no reason to make it easy on them. Nikki backed up to the barn door and dropped the loading ramp. The boys had her load secured in just a minute. They cleared the ramp as she was closing it. I asked the boys to wait in the barn, we would soon have things to carry to the shop. Topper asked, "Might we have the flying disc, while we wait?"

"Sure, Topper. I'll bring it out."

"Oh, sir, I thought you should know. We are equipped with limited stealth. If overhead observation is your only concern, the tarp is not necessary."

"Thank you, Topper. I'll remember that."

I got them the Frisbee, and made a mental note to pick up a few more when I was in town.

Soon enough, the delivery driver showed up. Snitz was happy with him for bringing new smells. We got him unloaded and underway. I commed Nikki.

"Everything go okay, Hon?"

"I think the Major expected you to fly it up. He acted disappointed when he saw it was me. I think he wanted to deal with someone without as much knowledge of regulations."

"Too bad for him. He give you trouble?"

"Seemed like he was surprised to see me, but other than that, he was by the book."

"Don't suppose those trackers were to let the pirates catch us while we delivered that saucer?"

"Gee, Caveman, it bugs me to think that way about somebody in the Patrol, but that fits the facts."

"Well, I bet Dingus will come back with a cure for that problem, or know how to fix it."

"That's a good bet. I can't get over how different he and Dad are."

"Don't know about that one. I'm guessing getting marooned does things to your outlook."

"Could be. Glad I don't have to find out. Did you just call to shoot the breeze?"

"Could you bring the freighter here when you come in? If we're going to be using it this much, I want to get it Snitz friendly."

"Open the barn, I'm almost there."

She ran it in, and I found an inspection bot. I popped the cover on the power core once she shut down. I started the bot and went to the truck to get some more rubber. When Nikki saw what I had, she asked, "What's that for, Caveman?"

"If I fasten it between the main case and these free hanging pipes, it keeps them from making noise. How did you think I quieted Dingus' saucer?"

"Didn't have a clue. I wasn't here. All it needs is to be kept from vibrating?"

"That's the way it seems."

"I think there's a better way, Bob."

"Uh oh, you called me Bob, I missed something easy, didn't I?"

"We have a spray mounting compound that will work for that. Holds great, and there's a solvent to take it loose if you need to."

"Sounds like great stuff. We have any?"

"Never heard of a shop that didn't keep some around. Let me check the inventory."

She found a case of the stuff and pulled out a can. It was sized for an inspection bot to use. She gave it to the bot, and messed with her watch. The bot scampered back into the guts of the power core. One of the boys bounced the Frisbee off the back of my head. Ornery bots, at least they would fit in around here. Looking innocent, Taz asked, "Will you join us, sir?"

It looked like Nikki had the situation well in hand, so I threw it back and joined their game. At this rate, we'd have to change the name of the place to Whammo Ranch. When the bot was through, I helped Nikki put the panel back in place. "You think we ought to do this for all the stuff we have flying? I wouldn't put it past the Major to leak it to the authorities that they need to look for ultrasound."

"I hate to think you're right, but it's cheap and easy, so why not?"

"You mind taking a bot or two with you when you take this back to John's, and taking care of the ones over there? I'll get these and put the boys back to work."

"Sure you will. How long are you gonna play Frisbee first?"

"No, really, we'll get right to work, won't we, boys?"

A chorus of, "Yes, Sir!" answered me.

"Why don't I believe any of you?"

"Good sense?"

Nikki gave me a kiss and a hug, and climbed aboard.

Contrary to Nikki's opinion, I pulled the access panels on everything we had running, and let the little bots loose with spray goo. I took the boys to the garage, and showed them the new parts. I explained they just needed to be stored out of the way for now, but they would be a fun project when the rest of the parts came in.

"Fun, sir? What is fun?"

"Enjoyment, Ozzie. Like the flying disc."

"Will the canine assist with this, also?"

"I wouldn't be surprised, Ozzie."

The boys moved the parts down to the shop, and got back to plumbing and wiring.

I went back to the barn and buttoned up the saucers as the bots finished with them.

Snitz and I played Frisbee in the front yard 'til Nikki got back. "I knew you would be doing that! Did you get any work done?"

"All the saucers are squared away, the Chevelle parts are in the shop, and the boys are back to plumbing and wiring. We got our chores done before we came out to play."

"Well, okay, I guess."

"You hungry?"

"I am, Caveman. You want to eat here, or what?"

"I need to run by and take some more training. You want to go to town while we're out?"

"That sounds good."

We locked up, and I called the boys and told them we would be away for a while. When we got to John's, he and Max were sitting on the porch, discussing something. "Hi John, what's up?"

"We were discussing waking Bill up tomorrow."

"Buzzkill!"

"You're telling me. You guys mind coming over tomorrow morning so we have more people to keep him contained?"

"Aw, Mom, do we have to?"

"Yes, Bob, yes you do.", Nikki said.

"Gee, I hope he at least wakes up in a better mood this time.", I replied.

John said, "You know his type. It was our fault he crashed. If Nikki hadn't bounced him, every thing would have been rosy. Besides, he had it all under control, even though he was unconscious and bleeding out."

Max spoke, "You boys have such a high opinion of human nature. You don't think he learned anything from the last time?"

Nikki said, "Not a thing. Didn't even wipe his logs before he crashed. He could have at least put the cause in doubt, but he didn't even try."

I said, "My vote is to call the sergeant before we wake him up, let them take care of him."

Nikki said, "He'll try to get us arrested, Bob."

"No way around that, is there?", I asked.

"I'll send his personal log to the Patrol, and to the sergeant, personally. It's all I can think of."

John said, "Wish Dingus was back."

Max retorted, "Why, so he could shoot Bill?"

I said, "No, Max, because he has pull, and can cover us when all this political crap starts."

Max looked a little frustrated, but he accepted that.

John asked, "What brings you to our fine establishment this evening, Bob? Trying to bum some supper?"

"Nope. We were planning to eat in town. I was thinking I should train some more. If Dingus gets back before I finish, my heinie is grass."

"Good thing the courier came with more Motrin today. Let's get you set up."

I came out of it a little confused, but things settled in quickly. I was getting used to the training machine. "So, John, what do I have left?"

"Looks like just that special that Dingus left for you."

"Maybe I should take it in the morning, get caught up."

"You think you need it to deal with whatever Bill throws at us, don't you?"

"I'd rather have it than not."

Snitz and Max were having fun, so we decided to pick Snitz up on our way home. Be more fun for him than sitting in the truck while we ate. We got to town before the rental place closed, so I rented a large truck, and asked if it was okay if I left it on the lot and picked it up after supper. They didn't have a problem with that. Then we hit the sporting goods place for an assortment of Frisbees. Gotta keep the boys happy and doing that good work.

After we got seated and got our drinks Julie came out to see us. She had on a business suit, instead of her uniform, and looked stressed. "Bob Wilson, what did I do to you? You wouldn't believe the amount of paperwork it takes to keep this place going. Why did you talk me into this?"

"You'll get the hang of it, Julie. You've been talking about your own restaurant since I've known you. You have a good crew, you just need to trust yourself."

"I know Bob, but I'm drowning in the business end. The customers, the kitchen, those things I understand. The paperwork and government stuff are going to make an old woman of me."

"Maybe that's what you need. An old woman, somebody who's already done all this crap and knows how to get it done. I bet Dee would know somebody."

"That doesn't sound as crazy as it ought to. But who knows when Dee will be back?"

"I'll call her." I got the call started before either lady could stop me. I heard, "Just a minute, Old Man, it's Bob. He wouldn't call for nothing. Hi Bob!"

"Hi Dee, hope I'm not interrupting anything. We're here with Julie. She bought the restaurant, and the business end has got her wrapped around the axle. We figured you probably knew someone who has been there and done that, who could help her out 'til she gets the hang of it."

"Is John handy? They keep her doped up more than they did me. She never really decided it was worth the effort to play their game."

"We're gonna have to bust her out?"

"If you want the best. Her name is Joanna Jackson. She doesn't have any family, so you're good there. Her arthritis is pretty bad, though."

"Okay. Thanks Dee, I'll see if we can get that taken care of. Enjoying the galaxy?"

"You could say that. Do you need anything else? I need to get back."

"Nope. Thanks, Dee."

"Later, Bob."

"See, Julie, no biggie. All we gotta do is kidnap a little old lady."

"Big Brass Ones, Bob. It's always simple with you, isn't it?"

"Try to keep it that way, if I can."

"How long is it going to take to arrange all this, you think?"

Nikki was working with her watch. I said, "I think we're about to find out." Nikki looked up at us watching her. "So I'm making the crazy plans now?"

"That wasn't what you were doing on your watch?"

"Well, yes, but I expected you to come up with something, too."

"Last time we hired a hacker to fake the records. If Mrs. Jackson doesn't have family, that's probably not going to work this time. I haven't come up with much yet. How 'bout you, Julie?"

"You know, Bob, up until the last couple of weeks, I thought you were a law abiding citizen, square as a cube. Funny how wrong a person can be. I don't have a thing. You want to know how to keep your tips off your taxes, I'm your girl. This is above my pay grade."

Nikki said, "I guess I'm driving then. Bob, you already rented that truck. That's for moving the rest of your tools, right?"

"Yes."

"You're doing it at night so the boys can help?"

"Yes."

"Those big windows at the home would be no problem for the boys to pop out and put back. All you would have to do is divert for a few minutes, and then go right back to moving."

"I like it so far, but John's autodoc is full."

"One of the saucers has a newer model on board, all ready to go. The bots just went over it. She won't make lunch rush, but I think we can have her here by supper."

Julie spoke up, "Who are these 'boys' you two are talking about? You think you can have Mrs. Jackson here for supper rush tomorrow? My brain hurts."

Nikki said, "The boys are three cargo robots Bob has adopted. Their names are Topper, Ozzie, and Taz. You should see them playing Frisbee with Snitz. I'm pretty sure Mrs. Jackson can be up and around tomorrow afternoon, unless there's something wrong with her we don't know about yet."

"You guys are nuts. Can I ride along?"

"We'll pick you up here when we get back to town. That work?"

"Yes."

We finished our meal, and I called John. "Hey partner, up for a little fun?"

"Good Lord, Bob. That's your 'pitching a caper' voice. Are you trying to scare me?"

"No, not at all. This one will be way easier than busting Dee out. No paperwork this time."

"That's called kidnapping, Bob."

"Dee's really sure the lady is tired of being doped up."

"You talked to Dee? Are they back?"

"Nope. Just called her to help with a problem for Julie."

"Julie's problem involves a raid on Shady Oaks? Things get complicated when you're around, Bob."

"Now you're just being mean. It's Nikki's plan."

"I feel SO much better now. I'll see if Max minds watching the autodoc. Will you be here soon?"

"Nikki has to drop me off, then she'll be right out."

Nikki dropped me at the rental, and we made plans to meet back at the restaurant. I ran home to get the boys. They had the lights on in the shop when I pulled up. I called and asked Topper to run the door up. "Sorry, sir, we are finishing the installation on the opener. It will be a few minutes before we can open the door."

"Can you leave it in the state it is in?"

"We'd rather not. Taz is holding the unit in place."

"Okay. I'll be right in."

I hung up and went in through the regular door. The boys all had their legs extended to work on the opener. I'd never seen them do high work before. I looked around, and saw that the shop was nearly finished. I wandered around, looking at all they had done. I heard the door start up, and Taz retracted to his normal height. He did a quick spin and then acted like he was panting. His imitation of his namesake was hilarious. I said, "You fellas have been accessing Earth media, then?". Topper said, "Yes. Is that unacceptable?".

"Not at all."

"Does our work meet your approval, sir?"

"No, Topper, it does not. It far exceeds any expectations I had. You boys are amazing."

"We have finished here. Should we return to the barn?"

"No, we need to go to town to pick up a few things. Could you fellas get in the truck, please?"

"Certainly, sir."

I turned off the lights and closed the door. They climbed into the truck, with Topper singing, "Lord, take me downtown, I'm just lookin' for some tush." I asked, "Okay, Ozzie, it's your turn. What do you have?"

"I'm going off the rails on a crazy train."

I laughed and pulled the door down. I knew I was in trouble as soon as they found Compressorhead videos on line.

I called Jack on the way into town. "Hi Jack, how's it going tonight?'

"It's a weeknight, so pretty slow. You do know I'm working tonight, don't you?"

"I was hoping you were on, but I didn't know for sure."

"More alien punks needing rescue?"

"Nope. Just need a favor, if you can."

"After that courier the other day, I'm motivated, Bob. How much jail time are we talking?"

"None, if Nikki's plan holds up."

"What do you need, then?"

"If you get a call out to Shady Oaks in the next hour or so, can you take your time responding?"

"Dee's got you busting out her buddies, now?"

"Something like that. Julie needs help running the restaurant. Dee recommended someone."

"They're back?"

"No. I called her."

"Do you really want to get on Dingus' bad side, Bob?"

"No, I do not. I'm working on a surprise for Dee that should get me back on his good side."

"You found her old car?"

"I did, but the fellow who has it doesn't want to sell. Dang near pulled a shotgun on me for asking. I'm building her a new one from scratch."

"You say this guy wanted to shoot you as soon as he met you? That's odd. Takes most folks a week or two."

"You're funny, but looks ain't everything."

"See ya, Bob."

"Later, Jack."

I met the rest of the crew at Julie's restaurant, and we drove to the closest parking lot we could leave a big U-Haul in without looking suspicious. The boys got out, and Taz said, "Sir, take these please." He handed me three ropes, each one tied around one of their necks. They used their arms as front legs, and turned on some kind of camo. Suddenly, I was walking three large dogs. I closed the door, and we went to meet the others. John said, "Nice dogs, Bob. Snitz get lonesome?"

Topper turned off the camo on his head and said, "Good evening, sir. You too look nice." Then he was a dog again.

John said, "How 'bout that? Bob's not just a bad influence on people. He corrupts bots, too."

Taz faded in, "He is not corrupting us, sir. Mr. Wilson is the nicest owner we have ever had. He has taught us the Frisbee." He faded out.

"Frisbee, Bob?"

"I don't have enough work to keep them busy all the time, they enjoy it." Nikki was on her comm. "Dee, it's Nikki. I need to know which room is Joanna's."

She counted windows, and said, "I think I have it. Is there some way to tell from outside the window if we have the right room?"

Nikki listened, and replied, "Got it. Can you stay on the line to talk to Joanna when we get in? Thanks."

Nikki led us to a window, and then got out her night vision and checked the room. "This is it. You're up, boys."

She must have downloaded what she wanted them to do, because they dropped camo and got right to it. Topper and Ozzie held the window with some kind of suction grippers, while Taz removed the frame holding the window in. Taz finished, backing out of the way. Topper and Ozzie pulled the window, moving to the side. Nikki and John went over the sill, and could hear Dee's voice calming Joanna. Shortly, John handed her over the sill to me, and they climbed back out. The boys reinstalled the window, and then John led the dogs back to the truck. I put Joanna in the back seat of Nikki's truck, and John crawled in the other side to start waking her up. I kissed Nikki, and got back in the U-Haul. When I got to the old place, the neighbor was walking his dog. I pulled to a stop and called out, "Just getting a few last things. I'll try not to make too much noise."

He said, "Sorry to see you go, Bob. You've always been a good neighbor."

I backed up tight to the old shop, so nosy eyes wouldn't see the boys doing their thing. I showed them what needed done, and mostly just stayed out of the way. Topper said, "All done, sir. Should we load up now?"

"We have a few more things to get. I'll need to back up to the house."

"We should ride in the truck, correct?"

"That would be right. Thank you, Topper."

We pulled both my safes, and I looked to make sure I wasn't forgetting anything. Then we loaded up and went home. I backed up to the big door, and the boys got to work unloading. Nikki walked up with Snitz. I asked, "Do you mind following me back in to return this truck? Tomorrow is going to be busy enough."

"Sure. Snitz will want to ride with you, though. He whined when I brought him here and he couldn't find you."

"No problem."

We dropped off the truck, put the keys in the drop box, and headed back. When we got in, Snitz had to check one more time to make sure his outdoors was in order.

Ear licking time was early, as usual, and I started coffee on the way out. Nikki was up when we got back. "Caveman, we need somebody to stay away from this meeting to be able to call Dingus if things go sideways."

"I agree, but I already told John I would be there. You know regs better than any of us. Maybe we could get your Dad to come over and stay with Snitz. When is Joanna supposed to wake up?"

"I set the doc to hold her 'til we woke her manually. I wasn't sure what might happen today, and I didn't want her waking up alone."

We ate, and drove to John's. Max was fine with not dealing with the Patrol, so Nikki took him and Snitz to our place. I got a call after they left, asking if there would be someone home to receive another delivery. I said yes, and then called Max to tell him to just have the driver put it in the garage.

Nikki got back, and John said, "Well, we're as ready as were going to get. Call the sergeant, Bob."

"Sergeant Darning? This is Bob Wilson. Young Bill is ready for a ride home, if you've got time to pick him up."

"Mr. Wilson, you always have the most cheerful news. I'll be there in ten minutes."

We waited five minutes, and then John and I went to wake him up. Nikki stayed to greet the Patrol. Bill woke, saw who we were, and sputtered, "You two again! Where is Ms. Slongum? I will have words with her."

John saw I wasn't going to be calm enough to do the talking, and said, "We saved your ass again, Buttercup. You might want to check your attitude. Your ride will be here soon. Get dressed, and we'll take you to meet it."

"My ride? What are you blathering about?"

"Your uncle is sending someone to pick you up. Your saucer was in pretty bad shape."

Bill lost some of his color. "My uncle? Why did you call him?"

"We didn't have contact information for anyone else. Is there a problem?" John was grinning at this point, since he knew Bill was in deep kimchee for coming to Earth without a valid permit.

Bill tried to play it off, saying, "Oh, no, no problem."

The wind out of his sails, Bill got dressed and we took him upstairs. Nikki was chatting with Sergeant Mike. "Oh, here they are. Sorry to have delayed you, Sergeant."

"No trouble ma'am, it was only a minute. How are you gentlemen?"

"Doing well. And yourself?", I replied.

"Another day in the Patrol, nothing special."

"Guess you have to get back? No time for coffee?"

"I've heard about this coffee, and I'd like to try some, but not today, I'm afraid. Things to do."

Bill really wanted to go off on Sergeant Mike for being so friendly with us, it showed all over his face, but he held his tongue. John said, "You really should come by sometime when you can stay for a bit. Maybe Sunday, we'll get you in on our paintball game."

"Sounds good, I'll let you know if I can make it. See you later."

When the saucer was gone, we all breathed a sigh of relief. Nikki said, "That was smoother than I expected. What did you two do to Bill?"

John said, "All we did was tell him we had called his uncle to pick him up. I guess that wasn't how he wanted to get home."

"You realize that means the Major will be forced to take official notice of the fact he was here without a permit, flying an unsafe saucer, right?"

I spoke up, "Aw, that's just too bad for young Bill, isn't it?"

She said, "Caveman, the Major isn't going to be happy we made him put his nephew in legal trouble. He will hold a grudge."

"Wasn't he already? The trackers on that saucer, weren't they for the purpose of giving one of us up to the pirates?"

"It does look that way, but this doesn't do anything to make things better."

"No, it doesn't. I don't know how else we could of handled it, though. Should we have patched Bill and his saucer up for free, and sent him on his merry way? We're already not getting paid for his time in the box. At least they paid up for hauling his clunker to the Patrol base."

"I don't think there was a good answer, Caveman."

John said, "Can't make everybody happy. I thought you were going to finish training before they got here, Bob?"

"Too much going on, I forgot. Better do it now, before something else happens."

Nikki said, "Call me when you need a ride, I'm gonna help Dad with that delivery."

She gave me a kiss and a hug, and drove off.

"She's right, you know, the Major is gonna want a chunk out of us for this.", John said.

"I know. If we had snuck Bill back without telling him, he would have been madder when he found out. At least this way, it looks like we respect his authority."

"You may be right. It's not something we can do much about, either way."

"Wish Dingus was here. He'd know what to do."

"Can't shoot everything, Bob."

After my training, I told John, "You should take this stuff, too. It teaches you how to deal with the faster reflexes, how to get the best use out of them."

"You think I've been slacking off? The hardest part is giving myself the shots. Max doesn't want to learn how."

"Surprise! Surprise!"

"Okay, Gomer, you want a ride home?"

"Thanks."

We had to park in the road, since the delivery truck was unloading. We went to see if we could help. The driver's pallet jack wasn't doing too good on gravel, but with all of us pushing, we made it. "Guess I better see about getting this drive paved.", I said.

The driver said, "Ah gee, just for me?"

"My crew is out of something to do for a couple days. Might as well, don't you think?"

"Bad enough you guys are in the middle of nowhere. Now you're comedians, too?"

Nikki said, "Oh, he was like this even when he lived in town. I think it's a birth defect."

John said, "Nah, just dropped on his head when he was a baby. Repeatedly."

The driver asked me, "These are your friends? How do people treat you when they don't like you?"

"They're not that bad. At least I know they're paying attention."

I tipped him for fighting the driveway, and he headed out.

I asked Nikki, "Do you think boys could make it look like blacktop? It would be nice to be able to unload without all the fuss."

"Other wives get presents. All I get is more work. I don't think you're doing this right, Caveman."

"Guess I need more practice."

John said, "How did bots turn into 'boys'?"

I answered, "They've just gotten a little more personality."

"Personality? Do I wanna know?"

"They've been accessing the internet, finding out things about their names. It's cool."

"I think I need to see this."

"Okay." I grabbed a couple of the new Frisbees, and let Snitz out of the house.

"C'mon, Max, fresh air and sunshine will do you good."

Max grumbled.

Nikki said, "Dad, it will be fun. Don't be a grump."

He got up and came along.

When we got to the shop, Taz greeted us with a spin and mimed heavy breathing. John lost it. "Taz, my man, that is right on. Give me five." He stuck out his hand. Taz froze for a second, accessing the internet. Then he lightly slapped John's hand. "You have brought more discs, and Snitz the canine. Is there to be fun, today?"

"Yes, Taz. Where are Ozzie and Topper?", I asked.

"They have yet to finish their instruments."

"Instruments?"

"Yes. Drums are easy. I'm already done."

John said, "Have they found Compressorhead?"

I answered, "It sounds like they may have. See now why I like to keep them busy?"
Nikki asked, "What is Compressorhead?"
John said, "An all robot band."
"They are going to make music?"
I replied, "They may need some practice before you can call it music, but they certainly have the right venue."
"Venue? What do you mean?"
"They're a garage band!"
John got out a Frisbee, and Taz said, "Could you please throw it to me, sir?"
John obliged, and Taz caught it with a spin. As he came around, he threw right over Snitz' head. It skipped, and turned into a floater for Snitz to chase. John said, "You guys have been practicing."
Taz said, "Yes, sir. We have become Frisbetarians. 'What goes around, comes around. When you die, your soul goes up on the roof, and you can't get it down.'"
John marveled, "Mac Davis? You fellas have been searching the net."
"We wish to 'fit in', sir."
"Keep it up, you'll fit in fine."
We showed Max how to throw, and played Frisbee 'til the sound of a guitar riff came from the back of the shop. Soon a bass joined in. Taz said, "I believe I am needed."
He trundled off toward the sound. Soon, 'Back in Black' filled the shop. I looked at John. "Beats a stereo!"
"Sure does!"
We threw the Frisbee around some more, enjoying the music and having a good time. When the boys played something danceable, I did my best to keep up with Nikki. Nikki's comm beeped, and she said, "Where did the time go? It's time to wake Joanna." She and John went to take care of that. I asked the boys if they would be able to do some work, since we had other places we needed to be. Topper asked, "Was our playing acceptable, sir?"
"Your playing was wonderful, Topper. I'm looking forward to hearing you again. We have more parts to move, and I want to get you started on putting things together." I had them bring the new parts and the donor car to the shop, and explained what needed to be done. Topper said, "If we have questions, we will get in touch, sir. There are more new parts coming, correct?"

"Yes. There is very little of the original car we will need to use."

As we were walking toward the house, we met Nikki and John helping Joanna get used to walking again. I asked, "How do you feel, Mrs. Jackson?"

"Pretty dang good, for an old woman. Soon as I get my balance back, I'll be fine. Oh, and it's miss, I never found a man who would put up with me."

"Can't imagine that, ma'am."

"You must be Bob Wilson. Delilah told me about you."

"Anything good?"

"Just to watch myself, because you are a smooth talker."

"Surely you're thinking of John here. He's the one always gets the women in bed."

Nikki slapped my arm. "That's because he's the doctor, asshole."

"You're a proctologist now, John?"

"I have to be, to take care of you."

Joanna looked at Nikki, "These two always like this?"

"No, ma'am. Mostly they're worse."

"I think I might like it here."

When we got to the house, I realized we hadn't had lunch. I asked, "Joanna, do you like chili?"

"I did, 'til my belly got old and picky. Bet I can handle it again."

I got out some I had frozen, and started it thawing in the microwave. She said, "Frozen chili? Ain't storebought, is it?"

"No ma'am. Had it in the crock pot all day before I froze it. Sometimes a body just don't have time to think that far ahead."

She looked at Nikki. "His eyes are brown, right?"

"Nope, they're blue. Delilah has accused him of wearing colored contacts, though."

"I bet she has."

I'd just gotten the chili on the table when my comm chimed. "Bob Wilson. How can I help you today, Sergeant?"

"I'm sending you a partial flight track. Our sensor guys think it's an equipment malfunction, but it sounds like somebody in trouble to me. Any chance you could check up on it?"

"Did our mutual acquaintances' uncle put you up to this by any chance?"

"No Bob, if he finds out where you got the track, I'll be cleaning johns for months."

"On it, Mike. I'll let you know what we find."

I asked the room, "Anybody up for a joyride?"

Joanna said, "I've got to be at work soon."

Nikki replied, "You can use my car. Just be easier on it than Dee."

"That won't take much. Hey, people know my old name. Who should I be?"

Nikki said, "Probably shouldn't change the first name, you're used to that. What does anybody think about a last name?"

John said, "If not Jackson, how about Michaels?"

Joanna said, "Michael Jackson, you went there?"

"You wanna be Jermaine?"

"I see your point. You need to comb your hair different."

Nikki said, "She'll fit right in."

She left for work, and the rest of us piled into John's Wagoneer to go to his place. I asked Max if he was coming this trip, since we had it quiet so Snitz could ride. He said we didn't know what we were going to be up against, and we should save Snitz' first flight for a time when things were more settled. Nikki said, You're probably right, Dad. Thanks for taking care of him."

We pulled in, and John ran in the house to grab his go bag. Nikki and I got the barn open and the freighter ready to fly. John came aboard and asked, "Why are we taking this big hulk?"

I said, "We might have to bring them in saucer and all. Better to have it and not need it, don't you think?"

"You're right, Bob."

"Can I get that notarized?"

"Get what notarized? What did you think I said, Bob?"

"That's what I thought."

Nikki came into the cockpit in uniform. "May I have the ship, Caveman?"

"I stand relieved, Space Cadet."

"Good. Now you two idiots go get your suits on."

John and I got dressed, and went back up to see if Nikki had found anything.

When we returned, Nikki said, "Okay, we're close enough to Mike's track, I'll crank the sensors. Wow, I see what he means. Faint, intermittent, barely there, but it does sound like someone in trouble."

"Can you tell where it's coming from?"

"Direction finding on an intermittent signal? I told you Caveman, our stuff is technology, not magic."

"So how do we find them? Wander around and hope the signal gets stronger?"

John wondered, "The way the signal fades and comes back is regular. Do you think they could be tumbling?"
Nikki replied, "That would make sense, but how does that help us?"
I asked, "All your ships are bare metal, right? Kind of shiny?"
Nikki said, "Yes, You guys have a plan, don't you?"
I said, "More like an idea. If we get between them and the sun, we might be able to see reflections as they tumble."
John said, "It's at least as good as wandering around hoping."
Nikki said, "Let's try."
Nikki put us where we thought we needed to be. Then she programmed the visual sensors to look for a flashing light. It took a little time, but an alert came up. Nikki magnified the area around it. "There! See that flash? That's not natural."
She moved us in the direction of the flash, slowly.
As we got closer, we could see it was, in fact, a saucer tumbling.
I asked, "Can you tell how many people are aboard?"
"There's an adult female, who seems to be in medical distress, and a female child. I'll try to raise them on comm."
I was glad I had taken the language course, but it was emotional to hear the little girl say, "Can you please help me? My Grandma is sick, and she bumped the controls when she fell. I don't know how to fly yet."
Nikki said, "You're doing good, Sweetie. I'm going to need you to do some things for me, so I can come and help. Do you think you can help me?"
"I, I think so."
"Is your Grandma still on top of the controls?"
"No. She fell down on the floor."
"So you can reach?"
"If I stand on the chair. Sometimes Grandma shows me the buttons to push."
"Okay, that's kind of what we are going to do, but I can't see you, so you have to be sure before you do anything."
"I don't want to make it worse."
"You won't, Sweetie. We are going to make it so we can come help your Grandma."
"I'll try."
"Good. Do you see a light flashing?"
"Yes."
"Just one?"
"Two. One is close, that I can reach, and the other is way at the top."

Nikki motioned me into the copilot's seat, and gave me control. Then she said, "Okay, do you see the button just below the flashing light that you can reach?"

"I see it. Should I push it?"

"Yes. That will let me drive your saucer."

The readouts on Nikki's side of the board suddenly changed. She was moving controls, but our ship didn't respond. Then I looked up and saw that the other craft was slowing its rotation. John said, "Looking good. Do we go across in our suits?"

Nikki answered, "No. Close the hatches to the payload bay, John."

John hurried off to do that. Nikki got the saucer stabilized, and set her board to autopilot. She said, "Caveman, I need your chair."

I got out of her way. She obviously had the situation well in hand. The last of the hatch lights turned green, and John reappeared. "All done, Nikki."

She replied, "I show all green. Well done." Nikki began to maneuver, but the main screen kept a view of the saucer. Her nav screen was replaced with a view of the cargo bay, with the hatch opening. Nikki spoke into the comm. "I'm going to bring your whole ship inside mine, okay? I'm flying both of them, so everything will be just fine. Hold your Grandma's hand and it will all be over soon."

"Okay, is it all right to be scared?"

"Of course, Hon. It's always okay to be scared. As long as you do what you need to do, it doesn't matter. You're doing fine. Just a little bit longer, and we'll come get you and your Grandma, okay? Stay where you are 'til we come get you."

"Okay, I can do that."

Nikki motioned me into the pilot's seat. She killed comms and said, "When I signal, sit it down and kill drive."

She turned the comms back on. "You still okay, Sweetie? I had to talk to my friend Bob for a minute. He's helping me."

"I'm fine. It looks like we're going inside a ship."

"Yes, you are. That's my ship." Nikki signaled, and I set the saucer down and killed the drive. She closed the hatch and began pumping air back in. She set a course for home, and said, "Your ship, Caveman."

"I relieve you, Space Cadet."

I sat down and watched all the pretty lights while the ship's computer took us home.

Nikki came back and said, "Bob, I'd like to introduce you to my new friend. Bob, this is Leelee. Leelee, this is Bob, my very good friend."

I said, "Hi, Leelee, it's nice to meet you."

She said, "Is my Grandma going to be okay?"

"Our friend John is very good at helping people who don't feel good. He will do his very best for your Grandma."

Nikki said, "Do you know what a dog is?"

"No."

"My dog's name is Snitz. He's about so tall, and furry. He likes it when you pet him, like this." She stroked Leelee's head. "And he likes to catch a Frisbee."

"Frisbee, what's that?"

"It's a round thing that you spin and throw all at the same time."

John came into the cockpit. "I got her stable, and into the autodoc on their saucer. You should probably head to your place, so we can put her in that better one Nikki found."

"I'll call the boys. They can get things ready."

Leelee said, "Who are the boys?"

Nikki answered, "They are silly robots who play Frisbee with Snitz and make music."

Soon enough we were home, and I was backing into the barn. The boys had moved the saucer with the good autodoc to the front, so John didn't have as far to move his patient. Leelee wanted to see her Grandma before she went back into an autodoc. John came out carrying her, with a blanket covering her. She was awake, and saw Leelee. "Leelee, honey, Grandma is going to be all right. This nice man is taking good care of me. I just need to go lay down for a while longer. You be good for these folks, okay?"

"Yes, Grandma. I hope you feel better soon."

"Me too, Sweetie. We need to finish our trip, don't we?"

John took his patient away for more treatment, and Topper came up to the cargo hatch. "Hello, sir, does this saucer need maintenance?"

"We should probably give it an inspection, while it's here. Have the little guys put in the sound insulation, also."

"If you would be so kind as to get off the ship, we can unload and begin."

"Sounds good. Once you get it moved, I'll start the diagnostics."

Nikki, Leelee, and I stood off to the side as the boys picked up the saucer and carried it to a parking spot. Leelee said, "They are strong. I thought you said they were just silly."

Nikki replied, "Not just silly, but they can be silly when they get through with their work."

Taz must have heard Nikki, because as soon as the saucer was securely in its new spot, he sped over and did his spin and pant routine. Leelee laughed. "He's funny."

John came out of the saucer and said, "She's all snug. Should be ready to come out by morning, I think, Robert."

Nikki caught the code this time. "Leelee, let's go find something to eat. I bet you're hungry."

When they were gone, I told John, "Step into my office", as I went aboard the saucer to start diagnostics.

John said, "Has Nikki scanned this?"

"No, I didn't realize that was necessary. Just a minute, I'll be done here."

I finished setting up the diagnostics I wanted, and made sure the boys had the smaller bots taking care of inspecting the saucer. Then John and I walked over to the other side of the barn. He said, "Leelee's Grandma isn't sick. She was poisoned."

"Any idea why?"

"She was still too weak to tell me much when I moved her."

"Maybe we'll get some answers when she gets out of the 'doc.", I mused.

"I hope so. Getting these adventures dropped in our laps gets old."

"I better call Mike and tell him how things came out."

I pulled out my comm, and hit Mike's code. He answered, "Sergeant Darning. Is my dry cleaning ready?"

"You can't talk?"

"That's right, I'll be by after my shift to pick it up."

"We found your sensor ghost. Grandma and a little kid. Grandma passed out from being poisoned. Knocked the saucer off course when she fell. You saved their lives, Mike."

"I see. I'll be sure and let you know if I need any more cleaning done."

He disconnected.

John said, "He was with somebody?"

"I think so. Maybe he'll call back when he's free. I'm gonna run over and get Snitz. Need a ride?"

"I'll come and grab a few things, but I better stay here tonight."

"No problem. Bob's Saucer Motel, plenty of room."

"Why do I get the feeling I can check out any time I like, but I can never leave?"

"Maybe it's your Eagle eyes."

"Ouch! Bob is sharp tonight."

I told Nikki where we were going, and we headed out.

Max was curious how things had come out, so I filled him in while John collected his stuff.

Max asked, "So you don't know anything about how these two came to be in the situation they were in?"

"Not yet. I'm hoping either the older lady or Mike can give us some idea just what's going on. Leelee isn't going to be much help there, I don't think."

"She might have seen something, but it's doubtful."

John was ready, so I said, "See you tomorrow, Max. Maybe we'll know more by then. Come on, Snitz."

We met Joanna as we were pulling out of John's drive. She asked, "Where am I staying? I never thought to ask."

"You any good with kids?"

"I do all right, why do you ask?"

"That rescue we went on. There was a little girl, and her Grandma is pretty sick right now."

"Sure, I can help. I'll follow you over."

When we all got unloaded, Joanna said, "Well, that was a welcome change. Sitting around doped up gets old fast. Hard to get my head around, though. Little Julie Butterfingers running the place."

I asked, "Julie Butterfingers, what now?"

"I trained her when she first started waitressing. She dropped more plates that first week than anybody I ever saw. If the customers hadn't liked her so well, the boss would fired her over it."

John said, "Do us a favor and don't mention that you told us that story, please?"

"Why not?"

"I think it might distract her for just long enough to get a shot off in paintball."

"Sneaky man. I like it."

Jack rolled up just then, in his civilian vehicle. "Hey Bob, is that the fugitive from geriatrics?"

I answered, "Sir, I have no idea what you're talking about. This is my old friend, Joanna Michaels. She's staying here a few days while she settles in to her new job."

"It's a pure miracle your eyes aren't brown, Bob. You're going to have to quit robbing the nursing homes for staff. People are bound to talk. This time you didn't even leave them any computer record she was ever there. That's just mean, Bob."

"Must have been Nikki that did that one. We didn't do any hacking. Come on in the house, we'll ask her."

Nikki and Leelee were on the couch, watching Taz cartoons. Every time he did the spin and pant, Leelee laughed. "Just like Taz the robot!"

I said, "Do you have time to meet some people, Leelee?" Then I realized I was speaking Galactic. I looked at Nikki. "Do we have a badge she can use?"

Nikki stepped in the other room and put one on Leelee when she came back. Leelee said, "Pretty. What is it?"

The kung fu movie effect got everyone's attention.

I said, "It's a translator, honey. Not everybody speaks Galactic."

"Oh. Okay."

"Leelee, this is Joanna. She's our friend, just like you. And this is Jack. He's our friend, too."

Leelee said, "Nice to meet you. Are you here to help my Grandma, too?"

Jack said, "No, Sweetie, I just came by to see Bob. I didn't know he had company."

Joanna said, "I'm not smart like John, so I can't help your Grandma. But I am good at cuddling and waiting. Do you need any help with that?"

Leelee said, "Maybe so. I'm not good at waiting, and I'm scared for my Grandma."

Joanna took over cuddling duty, and I motioned Nikki into the kitchen. Jack asked, "Nikki, did you erase all Joanna's records when you clowns broke her out?"

She answered, "I did. I thought it would make it harder for them to convince anyone she was really gone. Is it going to be a problem?"

"I don't think so, but if you guys need to bust out any more of Delilah's buddies, you need to find a way to leave a convincing paper trail that shows they transferred to a different place. Another case like this, and someone will take notice."

"I'll be more careful, Jack. I didn't mean to make trouble."

"I know, Nikki. You were just trying to help, and you did. I just wanted to warn you before you got in any deeper. I better get going. Paintball still on, Sunday?"

John answered, "You bet!"

Nikki asked, "How bad did I screw up, Caveman?"

"Not enough to worry about, but we might want to discuss messing with computer files before you do it, if it's not too much trouble."

"Sure, Caveman. I forget we're trying to keep all this quiet long term."

Joanna said, "Speaking of quiet, she's finally dropped off. Is there someplace we can sleep? I don't think her waking up alone in a strange place is a good idea."
Nikki and I said together, "Take our bed."
"Are you sure?"
I answered, "Yes. We've bunked in a saucer before. It's not a problem."
"Then can one of you big strong men carry her in there?"
I went to help.
"Gently, Bob, don't wake her."
There were a few grumbles and sighs, but I got her to bed without waking her.
I whispered, "See you guys in the morning, then."
The rest of us snuck out to the barn, and found places to sleep.
The lick on the ear came much sooner than I thought it should. I kissed Nikki's cheek, and got up to take care of business. Once we had found the plants in need of Snitz' services, I headed up to the house to start coffee. I didn't pay attention to where Snitz went. I was peering into the depths of my second cup, trying to discern the secrets of the universe in its swirls, when I heard, "Who are you?" in Galactic. Then, "Ooh, that's wet, stop!".
Snitz the canine alarm clock strikes again. Joanna was trying to explain to Leelee, but Leelee had taken her badge off to sleep, so no communicating was going on. I made it around the corner just as Joanna had figured out the problem, and decided she could do better talking to Snitz. "Get down, Snitz. Go lay down." Snitz hopped down, and found his place on the rug. I saw Leelee's badge on the night stand, and got it for her, while saying, in Galactic, "That's just Snitz. He thinks it's his job to wake people up in the morning."
"Is he an animal?"
"Yes, he is."
"Why is he in the house?"
"He lives with us."
"You live with animals?"
"Just Snitz. He's a dog. Our people have kept dogs for many years. They help us keep watch, and they are our friends."
Joanna said, "Snitz won't hurt you. He's a friendly dog."
I asked, "You folks hungry?"
Joanna said, "That coffee smells great, and then I'll think about food."
Leelee asked, "Can I have some more cereal?"
"Of course you can. I'll see you two in a little bit."

I went back to the kitchen. Zombie Nikki showed up, arms out, moaning, "Coffee, coffee."

I poured her a cup, and told her, "Leelee got Snitzed this morning. I don't think it's one of her favorite Earth customs, so far."

"She got the ear lick? Oh, no."

"She did. She seemed more concerned about the concept of animals in the house, than being licked by one."

I got started on breakfast, after I set out cereal and milk for Leelee.

She and Joanna wandered in, and my phone rang. Joanna took over breakfast, without me asking.

I answered, "Bob Wilson, how can I help you today."

"Mr. Wilson, I have a bunch of stuff on my truck for you. Will you be around to receive it?"

"There will be someone who can deal with it here all day. Do you have directions?"

"I still have the ones from the other day. Get that drive paved yet?"

"No sir, but if you pull around to my shop, we can unload on a hard floor. It wasn't quite finished the other day."

"I'll be there in about a half hour."

"See you then. Bye."

I called, "Come on, Snitz. Let's go see the boys."

We went down to the shop. Band practice was going strong. I hated to interrupt, but if the trucker saw them, the story would be all over the state by the weekend. Not the way to keep a low profile. Topper asked, "Sorry, sir, did we disturb you?"

"Not at all, couldn't even hear you at the house. I came to tell you that I need you to move to the barn and stay quiet for a while. The truck is bringing in the last of the parts, and I wanted to unload them here so you didn't have to carry them."

Topper said, "But sir, we learned a work song and everything." He cut down on a near perfect rendition of Cleavon Little singing 'I Get a Kick Out of You' with Ozzie and Taz doing the backup part. I don't think I was moving air for a good minute, I was laughing so hard. We left the big door up for the shipment, and wandered up to the barn. John was just stirring. My evil plan was moving apace. I said, "Boys, show John your work song."

I began to think my CPR lessons were going to come in handy, before John started moving air again.

"You, Bob Wilson, are an E-ville man."

"Hey, they got me first. Just spreading the love. There's coffee, unless Nikki drank it all."

Topper said, "Sir, you might want to see this."

He had the report the maintenance bots had compiled projected in the air in front of him. It showed sabotage remarkably similar to what Lyla had come in with. The little fellows had managed to weld it without pulling the part out.

"That's not good."

"Nor is this." He held out a tracker that looked familiar as well. "It has been deactivated, sir."

I announced to the room, "Good work, all of you. Damn fine work."

John and I went to the house. John did the coffee zombie entrance. Joanna cracked up, but Leelee was confused. Nikki tried to explain, but basically wound up at, "It's an Earth thing, you wouldn't understand."

Surprisingly, Leelee accepted that. I laid the dead tracker in front of Nikki. "The maintenance bots found that nasty little fellow in their saucer, along with sabotage that looked quite a bit like Lyla's saucer, it just hadn't let go yet."

Nikki pulled out her comm. I asked, "Who're you calling?"

"Lyla will want to know about this. You should call Mike."

I stepped in the kitchen and dialed. "Hi Mike, can you talk?"

"For a little bit. What's up?"

"That saucer you sicced us on? It was sabotaged like the reporter's was. It also was carrying a tracker. Either there are still pirates, or some of their sabotage hasn't let go yet. Thought that might be something you would want to know."

"Thanks. I have to go. Bye."

"Bye."

I heard an air horn, and went out front to guide him down to the shop. He backed in, and started using his Tommy lift to get things down. I wrestled the boxes out of the way. He said, "You weren't kidding about a brand new shop. What do you do for living? I need to change jobs."

"Had a rich uncle I had never even heard of. He kicked off, and left me a wad of cash."

"Nice work, if you can get it."

"That it is."

"Building up that Chevelle? Seems like you've got enough parts to build one from scratch."

"I do. I just bought that for a clean title. Probably use some of the window glass, if it's not too yellow."

"That would be the way to do it, if a fella had the bucks."

I tipped him, and he went on his merry way.

I ran the door down and headed for the barn. John was there, checking on his patient. He asked, "Could you have Nikki step out here? It's time to get her up."

"I will, but I have to get the boys started on something first." Seems they have better hearing than I gave them credit for, because when I turned around to call them, they were standing in front of me.

Topper said, "You have work for us, sir?"

"Yes, I do. The rest of the parts have arrived. Go ahead and finish the assembly. You already know what I want done. I'll send you files to show how the exterior should look. They're old, so they may need restoration before you choose exact color values. If you have any questions, do not hesitate to call."

"Okay, sir."

They trooped off, whistling the theme from 'The Bridge On the River Kwai'.

"I'll get Nikki."

I found the ladies on the couch, watching more cartoons. Snitz was in Leelee's lap. "Nikki, honey, John needs you for just a minute." I sat down on the couch to watch with them, when Snitz whined. "Joanna, don't let him out. He might get lost, he's not used to living here."

"What's going on, Bob?"

"We've got company."

My comm rang. "Bob Wilson. What can I do for you this fine day?"

"You could open the barn so I have a place to park, Bob."

"Hi Lyla. Barn's full. You'll have to park in the new shop. The boys will open up for you. See you in a few."

I commed the boys and told them to open the big door, and make sure enough floor was clear for a saucer to park.

Topper said, "No problem, sir."

I got up to go, and Leelee asked, "What's happening, Bob?"

"A lady has come to talk to you and your Grandma about your big adventure. I'm going to go meet her."

"Can I come?"

"Sure, Leelee and Lyla, that's not confusing at all."

Joanna held Snitz while we headed out.

Lyla flew close enough to ruffle Leelee's hair. She giggled. The door started down, and we went in through the regular one. The saucer faded in as we entered. The door opened, and Lyla came out, not looking as put together as she sometimes did. "I got here quick as I could, Bob. Oh, who's this?"

"Someone you're here to talk to, I think. This is Leelee. Her and her Grandma had a big adventure the other day. Leelee, this is Lyla. She's a friend to Nikki and me."

"Nice to meet you, Leelee."

"You too, ma'am."

"Leelee, can you show Lyla the way to the house? I need to talk to the boys just a minute."

"Sure, Bob."

Lyla said, "Wait, boys, who do you mean, Bob?"

I bellowed, "Topper, Taz, and Ozzie! Front and center!"

Of course, Taz couldn't resist a spin and pant on the way in. Leelee laughed, but Lyla was confused. I said, "Leelee can show you why it's funny up at the house. These are the boys. Topper, Taz, and Ozzie."

"You named your cargo bots?"

"Seemed like the thing to do, at the time."

Leelee said, "Come on, I'll show you the other Taz."

They left. I asked the boys, "This saucer still bothers Snitz. Can you bring one of the maintenance bots down here and get that fixed, please?"

"Yes, sir, no problem. Could we use the maintenance bots to help with the Chevelle?"

"Of course."

When I got back to the house, Joanna and Leelee were deep into the process of educating Lyla about Taz. Wondering why John and Nikki weren't back yet, I turned and headed for the barn. Snitz followed. We saw the boys leading a troupe of maintenance bots, whistling again.

I went in, and knocked on the saucer beside the door. A voice I didn't recognize said, "A gentleman does not rush a lady, when she is getting dressed, young man."

Nikki said, "You obviously don't know my husband, ma'am. He's a lot of things, but I'm not sure you could count gentleman among them."

"I'm sorry ladies, I seem to be lost. I was looking for the amateur table. I seem to have found the pro table by mistake."

The new voice again, "At least he knows when he's been whipped."

"Whenever you're ready, ma'am. There's a little girl who will be mighty happy to see you."

"I'll be happy to see her, too. How many primitive customs have you indoctrinated her with?"

"Let's see, there's cereal, and cartoons, and puppy dogs, oh, I almost forgot, dancing robots. We haven't had a chance to introduce the dreaded Frisbee yet."

"I thought your wife was exaggerating. I was wrong."

When we all went through the door, Leelee exploded off the couch. Luckily, Snitz had already jumped off her lap to check out the new person in his house. "Grandma!! You're okay!"

"Yes, Leelee, I'm okay. Can you introduce your friends?"

She tried to bring Snitz over, but he was planted, looked at her Grandma with a head tilt and a puzzled expression. I said, "Nikki, could you scan please?"

She said, "Sure, Bob", looking at Snitz with concern on her face.

She waved her scanner around, and said, "It's this pendant, Bob. It's putting out weak ultrasonics."

I asked, "Ma'am, why is your pendant powered?"

Leelee said, "Be careful, I touched that right before Grandma got sick."

Grandma said, "I don't understand."

John ordered, "Ma'am, stand very still. I'm going to ease your jacket off, and then we'll have a look at your pendant." John first pulled the lapel with the pendant away from her body. A little needle was sticking out the back of it. John said, "Bob, is there a bar of soap handy?"

I went and got one. He said, "Carefully, jab the needle into the soap so it's not poking out anymore."

I did, and he finished removing her jacket. He said, "That's a nasty little trinket, ma'am. Where did you get it?"

"I've had it for years, I don't understand."

Nikki looked at me and said, "Call Mike. Now!"

I pulled my comm and dialed. "You must have the wrong number. I've already picked up my dry cleaning."

"Listen, Mike, that lady we saved had a rigged piece of jewelry. It just tried to kill her again. We got it before it could. This needs Patrol oversight, the sooner the better."

"I'm putting you on speaker. Can you tell the whole story?"

"Sure. The sergeant called us because he was worried a faint contact that you folks had dismissed might actually be someone in trouble. We investigated, and found a saucer tumbling out of control, with an unconscious woman and her young granddaughter aboard. My wife was able to talk the little girl through giving her remote access to the saucer's controls. She was able to bring it aboard our freighter, where we administered medical aid to the older woman. Upon returning home, we continued medical assistance. The autodoc concluded she had been poisoned. Upon being revived, she once again donned her clothes, to include a jeweled pendant. Our dog, who is sensitive to ultrasound, alerted on the pendant. Further examination showed a needle protruding from the back of the pendant. We have safed the needle, and the granddaughter has stated that she touched the pendant just before her grandmother became ill. Does that explain the situation?"

The Major's voice came over the comm. "It does Mr. Wilson. Do you have anything to add?"

"Only that during servicing the saucer, my maintenance bots found both sabotage and a tracker very similar to what was found on the saucer of Lilacrious Bongwater, when she was nearly killed."

"We only have your testimony for those events, they are of no consequence."

Lyla spoke up, "Major, this is Ms. Bongwater. Not only do I have recordings of the events in question, I have made statements about them on the record, with a scan running for truth, at your headquarters. Do you propose to question that?"

"No. I do not. I will have an investigator there within the hour. Goodbye."

Nikki spoke up, "Bad news, gents. They're going to want truth scans on all of this, and they are not going to allow any muscle relaxers."

I said, "At least Joanna wasn't here for much of it. Maybe she'll be able to go to work. The rest of us won't be good for much, I'm afraid."

John said, "I can always give the shot afterwards, Bob. Won't be quite as nice, but you won't be out of it all day."

"That sounds like a plan, John. Do you have enough in your go bag?"

"I do. It seems to be in demand, lately."

Snitz started whining. The saucer landed right out front. The investigators climbed out with some equipment cases, and it left again. Snitz calmed down, at least until the people from the Patrol came in. They smelled odd, I suppose, but he didn't think they needed to be in his house. I managed to calm him down, but he went in the other room. I said, "Sorry about that, usually he's better with strangers than that. How do you want to proceed?"

"We will need copies of any certified records of events, and testimony of all witnesses, to be given under scan."

"I understand. Lyla, Nikki, if you ladies could give these folks the copies they need? I have a favor to ask, if I may?"

"You may ask."

I pointed out Joanna. "Could you please take her testimony first? She has someplace else she needs to be."

"That is acceptable."

We all waited on the porch while Joanna was questioned. She came out, and said they wanted Nikki next. John gave her a shot, and she took off for the restaurant. Leelee's Grandma spoke up. "You folks saved my life, twice, and I don't even know your names. I'm Gennous Taurum."

I said, "Bob Wilson."

John said, "John Branham."

Lyla said, "Lilacrious Bongwater."

I said, "My wife, Benikkious Slongum, is inside."

Gennous asked, "The lady who had to leave?"

I said, "She is Joanna Jackson, but she's going by Joanna Michaels, now, though. Would it be acceptable to call you Genny? Galactic names are a little tough for us primitive types."

"Genny would be fine, yes."

Nikki came stumbling out. I jumped up and caught her before she fell. "Light her up, John. She's in a bad way."

John quickly drew the injection and administered it. "That should kick in a few minutes, Nikki. Try to get comfortable.", John advised.

The investigator who followed Nikki out asked, "What are you doing? What did you give her?"

John squared up to him and said, "We were just fixing the headache all your equipment seems to cause. The only reason we didn't prevent it in the first place, is because Nikki said you would get all high and mighty about us taking meds before answering your questions. All that was in the shot was a simple muscle relaxer."

"You can be next, for your attitude."

John turned to me and said, "5cc, Bob, 5cc".

I repeated, "5cc. Got it. 5cc."

"5cc, what code is this? Are you trying to beat the machine, you primitive idiots?"

I replied, "John is our medic. I know enough to help, but I don't know enough to decide dosages. He was telling me how big a shot to give him when he gets back. Nikki already told us there's no way to beat your machine, and we don't need to in the first place, since we've done nothing wrong."

"We'll see about that!"

I sat down and waited, figuring I was next. Genny asked, "These investigators don't seem inclined to take your word for anything. Is there a reason for that?"

"Their Major's nephew managed to get himself in some trouble on this planet. They blame us."

"That's Major Rottum? So you're speaking of Bill, his sister's boy?"

"I don't know how they're related, but his name is Bill."

"Not one of the better representatives our civilization could have sent."

I saw Snitz through the screen door. He was trying to get to the front door, but he didn't seem to want to come past where the scanner was running. Nikki was beginning to look alive again, so I asked, "Space Cadet, how are you feeling?"

"Good enough not to stun you for asking, but it's a near thing. Give me a few more minutes and I'll be functional. You need something, Caveman?"

"You have your scanner with you?"

"Yes. Why?"

"Snitz doesn't like the truth machine."

"Oh. OH! I'll look, Caveman, I'll look."

She got it out, and took a reading. "Caveman strikes again! I wonder if the teaching machines are the same way?"

"We'll have to check when we can. Oop, here comes John."

I drew 5cc of medicine, checked for air, and unwrapped a wipe. John was unsteady, so I helped him sit, and proceeded to give him his shot. I put the cap back on the syringe, like John had taught me, and put everything in the used compartment on his bag. I stood and said, "I'm next, I assume?"

"Get in there, smartass."

When we got in the house, I asked, "Could you turn off your machine for just a minute? My dog wants out."

"What does the machine have to do with that?"

"Turn it off and see."

His partner wasn't as convinced we were guilty of something, I suppose. She flipped the switch. Snitz ran for the door, and I let him out.

"What does that prove? Just a trick you trained him to do, no doubt."

"Could be, or it's possible your machine is putting out an awful racket in the ultrasonic range. I'd bet a quarter ounce that's what causes the headache."

"Silly primitive! Come and get what you deserve."
The operator had a thoughtful look on her face, however. She said, "Sir, it's possible he's correct. The reports say that animal of his can tell when a saucer is coming."
"Those reports are all fiction concocted to keep the authors out of the brig. Operate the device and keep your opinions to yourself."
I sat down, and she placed the headset on me. It was different than either of the other headsets I had seen. It had more pickups than the one for acceptable contact, but fewer than the teaching machine. The questions went on for what seemed like a long time. We went over and over the same topics, with slightly different wording. Finally, Torky (They had never told me their names, he seemed like a junior grade Torquemada), said, "I don't believe it. Run a medical scan, they have some drug that allows them to lie to the machine."
She ran every scan she had. Twice. "He has a little caffeine in his system. Other than that, clean as can be."
The headache was fascinating. I hadn't realized I could hurt that much and not die. Torky threw me off the chair. "Get out! Send in Mrs. Taurum, and make it quick!"
I found standing was not in the cards at that point, so I crawled out the door, and moaned, "Genny, they want you."
John stuck me, and I must have passed out. The next thing I remember is Nikki standing up to them, quoting regulations about how they weren't allowed to question Leelee without an adult present. I rolled over and said, "Even us primitives have more morals than to browbeat a little kid into making stuff up."
I knew Nikki and Lyla would be recording. I figured I had just bought a get out of jail free card, since Torky would kick the crap out of me. To my surprise, he didn't. "All right, she can have one adult with her."
Leelee looked at me, and saw I was still in bad shape. Her next choice shocked everyone on the porch. "I want Lyla. She knows about asking questions." I was afraid Torky would stroke out. He had obviously avoided questioning Lyla, because as a reporter, she was always recording, even when she didn't look to be. To have her as Leelee's advocate would ruin whatever scheme he was trying to run. I saw his face change, and said, "Nikki, catch Snitz. He's about to call his ride."
"How do you know that, primitive!?"
"It's called poker. You shouldn't play, you wouldn't be very good."

John cleared his throat, trying to keep from being obvious as he held in a laugh.

Torky hit a button on his watch, and stuck his head in the door. "Ensign, pack your gear! We are leaving immediately!"

"Yes Sir!"

As he turned around, their saucer reappeared. It couldn't have been far away. Then the overpowering stench of guano hit us. I knew I shouldn't, but my mouth outran my brain again. "Hid it in a cave, did you? That's those ultrasonics you don't believe in. Annoys the bats."

Torky stormed off, minion in tow. She turned and gave us an apologetic little smile, and then followed him aboard.

As I looked around, I remembered Genny had gone after me. I asked, "How's Genny?"

"I'm fine, Bob. They didn't question me very long. I also have prosthetic ears. They filter that noise you were talking about."

"That's great! I'm glad they decided not to question Leelee."

Nikki said, "Me too. Feeding her cereal, Bob? They would run you in for child abuse."

"Probably. Nobody is going to want to cook after the day we've had. How about we pick up Max and see how Julie and Joanna are doing?"

The unorganized chorus was generally in assent, but Nikki looked at me and said,"Bob" and then her lips kept moving.

"Oh crap, you two don't know English. Your badges will be noticeable, and we'll draw attention."

"I thought you boys had painless training down to a science. Light me up, John.", Genny said.

Leelee said, "Yah, me too, light me up."

I asked Nikki, "Those saucers in the barn have trainers, don't they?"

She answered, "Sneaky Caveman good. I keep."

I noticed I had a message waiting on my comm. It was from Topper, a list of paint colors and quantities. He also listed a gun and tips, and said he had found a local store with them in stock. He also wanted masking tape in various widths and a roll of paper.

I told John, "Sounds like Topper is ready to paint the Chevelle."

"Already? Those boys are good!"

"Don't know what I would do without my crew of illegal aliens."

John let that cook a second, and replied, "They don't have paperwork, do they?"

"Nope."

John and Nikki got Genny and Leelee going. Nikki stood next to the machine, running scans. I decided to go from the other side of the problem, and pulled up the schematics for the training machine. We found it almost together. Nikki came over to me and said, "Caveman, I found it."
I showed my search and said, "This piece right here?"
"Snagfart! You found it too!"
"I need help with something else, though. Can you show me how to forward this text to my phone, so I don't have to pull my comm out in the store?"
"Sure. Just pull up this screen, hit local, and put in your number."
"Thanks. How long 'til they're done?'
"Another five minutes or so, why?"
An enthusiastic kiss answered that. We were still at it when Leelee said, "Eww, kissy face!"
"I guess she's done", I said.
"Snagfart", Nikki whispered.
I needed my truck to carry home Topper's shopping list, but we wouldn't all fit. Nikki called Max and asked him to open the barn, and she flew everyone over in one of the extra saucers. I went on to town, hoping to get my shopping done by the time they made it to the restaurant. Since Topper knew exactly what he wanted, and had checked online to find who had it in stock, my shopping went quickly. They were still waiting on me when I got to Julie's.
Nikki said, "Come on, Caveman, we want to eat this week."
"Can't we put it off 'til next? I'm still full from breakfast."
"Ha, ha."
Lyla said to Leelee, "They're funny, aren't they?"
"Looks aren't everything."
That one stunned me. I did the only thing I could think of, and held out my hand for Leelee to give me five. She did, and smiled. "Lyla taught me that. Did I do it right?"
"Perfect."
Julie greeted us at the door. Nikki, John and I all got hugs. "Joanna is a Godsend. You three saved the day again. We're all going to pitch in and buy you capes."
Nikki, in a perfect Edna Mode voice, said, "No capes!"
John tried to play it off as a cough. I bit my lip. Then Julie lost it, and we were all laughing hysterically. Nikki joined in. Lyla, Genny, and Leelee

looked at Max. He said, "It's probably a reference to an Earth movie, knowing them. They can explain it when they calm down."

Once we got sat down, Nikki said, "I think you could understand better if we watched the movie when we get back. It's going to lose a lot if I try to explain it."

Julie and Joanna came out to our table. Joanna said, "We've been talking."

I interrupted, "Why do I have a sudden desire to find a phone booth?"

She came back with, "It's not that bad, Bob. We were just wondering if there was any way we could help the rest of the folks up at Shady Oaks. I'm really grateful for what you've done for me, even if it was just to help Butterfingers, here. I'm sure Delilah is grateful, too. But there are more people in that joint that could be useful if they just had the opportunity. At any rate, they deserve better than being doped up all day."

I got serious, "We can't bust them all out. Jack has already warned us people are getting suspicious."

"Surely there's something you can do?"

"They dope people because they don't have enough good staff, right? That's because they're trying to turn a profit. I wonder how hard it would be to buy the place and set it up with a decent operating budget and better oversight?"

"You would do that? For a bunch of old fogies?"

"If you and Dee are any indication, I need those folks to help me out. It's all self interest, Joanna. Just Bob looking out for Bob. I ain't no hero."

"You believe whatever you need to believe, Bob Wilson. You're still my hero."

Nikki purred, "Easy there. He's taken."

Joanna replied, "Lucky you!"

Max was trying to explain to our visitors from out of town, but he didn't seem to be making much headway. Nikki said, "I'll explain, but can it wait 'til we're done eating? I'd rather not talk about it in public."

They agreed, but of course, Leelee had a hard time being patient. Julie brought her out some crayons and a coloring page. It seems applying colored wax to paper is not something that is done in Galactic civilization. Leelee was thrilled. We promised to pick her up some crayons and a coloring book on the way home.

John asked if he could ride back with me, he didn't seem interested in helping Leelee choose a coloring book.

I think he just wanted to see how the boys were coming on the Chevelle. I know I did. We got to the shop, and I tried to run the door up. Nothing happened. I called Topper. "Yes, sir, what can I do for you?"

"The door won't run up, Topper."

"Yes. We disabled it to avoid dust in the painting area. Sorry, sir, should have informed you."

"No problem, Topper, that makes good sense. Glad to see you taking such precautions to make sure the paint comes out right. We're outside with the stuff from your list. Can we come in?"

"Certainly. Do you need one of us to carry things in?"

"John is with me, we can manage."

We took Topper his supplies. What we saw when we got inside was nothing short of amazing. The boys had done a beautiful job so far. We ogled it for a minute or two, and then Taz asked, "Did we make a mistake, sir? We studied everything we could find. Is it not good enough?"

John said, "Taz, it is beautiful, we are just admiring the quality of your work. Human workmen would have taken months to do this well."

He got a spin and pant as a reply. John held out his hand, and Taz gave him five. Six actually, since the bots had thumbs on both sides of their hands.

I said, "We'll get out of your way now. I'll give you some warning when we need to get this saucer out of here."

Ozzie said, "Thank you, sir."

John and I went to his place, and I dropped him off. I advised him, "You might hold off on ordering any more Motrin. Nikki and I have an idea cooking that might get rid of the need."

"What? You've actually fixed the machine so it doesn't cause headaches? That's going to be huge!"

"I said cooking, not ready to rock. We've got a good lead, but we still have to run some tests."

"Still, that's a biggie. Maybe we can get some respect from the Galactics if we fix that for them."

"The Patrol doesn't even believe their equipment puts out ultrasound. They're going to ignore whatever we say."

"Get Dingus to tell the Guide. He knows we know what we're talking about."

"Good idea. I'll do that if it works."

I got back before Nikki, so I pulled out my comm and looked through the inventory of the tools we had brought back. I found a gadget that would fix the issue Nikki and I had found. Since Topper had organized the barn, it was easy to find the tool I was looking for. I went to the saucer Nikki and I were sleeping in, and fixed the teaching machine. As I was walking back to the house, John pulled up and dropped off the ladies. He waved and drove off. Snitz ran to greet me. I bent down to pet him, and rose to find Nikki standing in front of me. I did what came naturally, and a shout of, "Eww, kissy face!", was heard.

I said, "She's cute, but that's unhandy."

Nikki said, "Nobody ever said it wasn't gonna be semi-tough."

I didn't move any air for a little bit. When I got done laughing, I had to wipe my eyes. "You got me good, Space Cadet. I wasn't expecting that."

"You have met my dog Payback?"

"When's she gonna have those puppies? If you start 'Incredibles', I'll make popcorn."

"Deal, Caveman. What were you doing in the barn?"

"The Watusi? I was trying that fix we figured out for the training machine."

"Did you test it?"

"I didn't want to be by myself, in case it didn't fix the headache."

"Good plan. You feeling okay, Caveman?"

"You're running short on tickles, you say?"

"Behave. We have company."

They got started on their movie, and I sat down to see what the internet could tell me about buying a nursing home. It didn't take long to figure out I needed to call our lawyer in the morning. Snitz came and rubbed my leg, and I took that to mean that the outdoors needed inspecting. Always vigilant, our Snitz. My comm beeped, so I answered. "Bob Wilson, what can I do for you this evening, Mike?"

"Bob, I have someone here who would like to talk to you. Is that okay?"

"Depends who it is, I suppose."

"Ensign Whittum, she was at your place this morning."

"She seemed like a decent sort, put her on."

"Mr. Wilson?"

"Yes, Ensign?"

"I wanted to apologize for what happened today. The Captain was out of line."

"Not your fault. He was in command. Why does he dislike us so?"

"Major Rottum sent him with instructions to find evidence of wrongdoing on your part. He was quite frustrated you were all 'straight arrows', I believe you say."

"That's what I had assumed. Hope we didn't get your Captain in trouble. He was following orders."

"He requested a transfer. He doesn't want to work for Major Rottum any more."

"That's a shame. He seemed like a good man, caught in a bad situation."

"You're very kind, after the way he treated you."

"Not his fault Major Rottum has it in for us. I will treasure the look on his face when your saucer arrived covered in guano. I'm not that nice."

"Fair enough. It seems you and Sergeant Darning have a sort of back channel network going on. It's already helped people, and I doubt that will stop. I was hoping I could be included?"

"Well, Ensign, considering who you work for, that could seriously endanger your career. Are you sure about this?"

"I am, Mr. Wilson."

"Call me Bob, then. You can get my comm code from Mike. Will you send me yours?"

"No problem. Is there anything we could do for you this evening?"

"Can't think of a thing. Have a nice evening."

"You too. Goodbye."

"Goodbye."

Snitz had finished his inspection, and I didn't want to bother Topper while he was painting, so we went back in the house. Their movie was finishing up. Leelee ran up to me and hugged my knees. "I won't tell your secret identity, Caveman."

I laughed so hard, Lyla and Genny looked like they thought Leelee had broken me. I picked up Leelee and swung her around. "You can fly! Are you a superhero?"

"You're silly, Bob."

Genny said, "I think it's time we found a bed, little one."

"You can take ours.", Nikki said.

"Where will you sleep?"

"In a saucer, like last night."

"Our saucer is cleared, isn't it?"

"Clean diagnostics and a physical inspection. Doesn't get much more cleared than that."

"We can sleep aboard, then."

Lyla spoke up, "I can sleep aboard as well, my saucer is well equipped."
I said, "Sorry, but no. The shop is in the middle of a critical operation, and the boys can't be disturbed until they are through."
Lyla gave me an odd look, "Okay, Bob? What's up?"
"It's a secret, and you're in the business of telling secrets. Better you don't know. I'm sure you'll find out next time you are here."
"Baawwwb, you're such a meany!", said Lyla and Leelee in unison.
"Sorry, can't be helped."
Tires crunched gravel, and I remembered Joanna needed a place to sleep. She came in, looking a little tired. "Wow! It's good to feel useful again."
I said, "Hey Joanna, Have a good day?"
"Best one in years. Thanks, Bob."
"Thank Dee when you see her. It was her idea."
"And you just went along because Butterfingers was in over her head. Don't those contacts get itchy after so long?"
"Believe what you want to believe, you will anyway. We were trying to figure out where everyone is going to sleep. Nikki and I are back in the saucer, Genny and Leelee are going to be in their saucer, that just leaves Lyla and you."
She looked at Lyla. "You snore?"
"Nope"
"Wanna share?"
"Okay."
"I need a shower. I'll be a few minutes."
"See you then."
We all wandered off to our chosen places. I was slightly delayed, because Snitz had duties to perform.
Snitz and I got in our saucer, and shut the door behind us. Nikki held up a syringe. "John gave me a dose, just in case. He said you wouldn't be able to wait to test the machine."
I kissed her and said, "You guys take such good care of me. Wish I deserved it."
"Sure you don't need to rinse those contacts, Bob?"
"Okay, I get a few things done. Do we have any training for unarmed combat? Dingus has me squared away with weapons, but I need more than what I learned in gradeschool for unarmed."
"We have a winner! Dingus said that would be what you looked for next. He left this."
She held up a training chip.

I sat down, and Nikki hooked me up. I said, "Here goes nothin'", and flipped the start switch.

I woke up less woozy than usual, but I could tell the training was still fitting into what I already knew. Then I remembered I should have a headache. Gingerly, I moved my head around, trying to see if tight muscles were waiting to trigger when I moved. I couldn't find any. Nikki asked, perturbed, "Well, Caveman, did it work?"

"Yes, it did. I just wanted to be sure before I said anything."

"That's great! Now people can learn without dreading it."

"We should call your Grandpa."

"Why him?"

"He can get the Guide using our fix. You don't think the Major would listen to us, do you?"

"No, he wouldn't. You could tell Mike, though."

"I could. I forgot to mention, that Ensign that ran the tests this morning, wants to be on our call list too. I'll send you her details."

"When did you find that out?"

"I was walking Snitz, during the movie. Mike called, and put her on. The major had ordered the Captain to come back with evidence against us. He couldn't find any, and that's why he was so upset. She said he put in for transfer, so that he doesn't have to work for Rottum any more."

"I can see why you didn't want to air all that out in front of everyone. The Ensign's career is done if the Major finds out she put herself on our call list."

"That's what I told her, but she insisted."

I dialed Dingus', and he answered, "This better be good, Bob Wilson."

"No training headaches, no drugs, one simple modification to the machine that takes maybe fifteen minutes if you have trouble finding your tools. Good enough?"

"Shocked as I am, I think I'm glad you called, Son."

"It's the same kinda deal as the power cores. There's an ultrasonic rattle that stresses you out. I just trained with it, no drugs, and I'm fine. Do you still have connections in the Guide?"

"I manage. What are you thinking?"

"I send you the file that shows how to fix it, and you give it to the Guide. The Patrol isn't going to pay any attention to me, not with Major Rottum in the chain of command. If the Guide gets good use out of it, it's bound to spread in society, right?"

"Don't you want to get paid?"

"Dingus, I already have more money than I know what to do with."
"Has Rottum pulled something else?"
"We rescued a lady and her granddaughter after the Patrol decided their distress call was just noise. He sent investigators to try and prove we did something wrong. Questioned us under truth scan, no drugs. I couldn't stand up when they got through with me. Lyla got most of it recorded. Should make a whale of a story."
"I should know better than to worry about you, but I still do."
"Any luck getting us set up as Guide auxiliaries?"
"I got you a full med pack and official mention as a fallback point. If this mod works out, they'll want to move the headquarters there and build you a statue."
"Aw, Dingus, you say the nicest things. I better go."
"Me too."
I turned to Nikki, "I believe there was a small matter of kissus interruptus?"
Roll call for outdoor patrol came early, as usual. Once we had determined that all was well with our corner of the world, and found the plants needing water and fertilizer, we headed up to the house. I started coffee. I heard the shower running, and then Lyla wandered out. "Do you think I can get some fresh clothes, Bob? Or is your secret project still going?"
"Don't know. I'll check."
I called Taz, not wanting to bother Topper if he was still painting. "How can I help you, sir?"
"The lady who owns that saucer needs to get aboard and get a change of clothes. Is the project still dust critical?"
"No, sir. We dried it with infrared light. You should come see it. Topper was able to match the pictures very well, I think."
"Could you put up some sort of barrier so that the lady getting in her saucer doesn't see your work? I'm worried she might spoil the surprise."
"We will have that in place by the time you arrive, sir."
I told Taz, "It's all good." Then I asked Lyla, "Mind if I walk down with you?"
"Okay. Do I get to see the big secret?"
"Will you promise not to tell anyone what you see until after the secret is revealed?"
"You're no fun, Bob. Okay, I promise."
I called ahead. "It's okay, boys, she promised me she wouldn't tell."
"If you're sure, sir."

"I am."

We started around her saucer, and Lyla said, "What's the big secret, Bob? Oh! It's beautiful! What is it?"

"1968 Chevrolet Chevelle, with modifications. Mostly a replica of Dee's old car, but with more modern parts."

"You made this for Dee?"

"No, the boys did all the work. I just showed them what needed to be done."

"But it's for Dee?"

"Of course."

"And I can't tell her?"

"Nope."

"Because it's a surprise?"

"Yes."

"And you showed me anyway?"

"Yes."

"Asshole!"

"You asked."

I called the boys over. "You three have done a magnificent job. This car is beautiful. What can I do to thank you?"

Ozzie said, "Drive her hard, sir. She's built to run."

"Can you fellas move the saucer to the side when she gets through in there? I'll need to take this beauty to town later and get some papers for her."

"Sure sir."

Lyla come out with an armload of stuff. I asked, "You need help with that?"

"I've got it. You ready to go back?"

"I am."

We headed back to the house, but Nikki was coming out of the barn when we got that far. I said, "Space Cadet, you need to come and see something."

"But, coffee."

"Better than coffee."

Lyla said, "Go see. It's beautiful."

When we got inside the shop, Nikki said, "This is beautiful! You boys did great!"

A chorus of "Thank you, ma'am", erupted from the boys.

She turned to me, "Caveman, she'll love it. Is it fast?"

"I haven't driven it yet. We'll find out after breakfast."

Joanna and Lyla were cooking when we got back to the house. Genny and Leelee got there not long after Nikki and I. Genny said, "It is nice spending time with you all, but we should probably get back to our trip today. How much do I owe you, Bob?"

I asked, "Lyla, what do you think? I always price things too low."

"Well, Genny didn't require emergency surgery, they didn't come in on fire, and so far they haven't drawn attention from any pirates. Cheaper than my bill, I think."

Nikki said, "We did have to go fetch them."

Lyla replied, "That's true. Three ounces sound fair to everyone?"

Genny tinkered with her watch to convert ounces to Galactic. "Oh, my! You'd let me off that cheap for saving my life? Twice?"

I answered, "We've got our prices low to get customers coming in. Once we get a steady business built up, we may raise them a little. Of course, there is a catch."

"What's that?"

"Leelee hasn't learned Frisbee yet. You'll have to stay the morning and play Frisbee with us to get that price."

"You drive a hard bargain, Mr. Wilson."

After we had eaten, we all trooped down to the shop. Band practice was in session. They were trying to fit Chevelle instead of Camaro into the lyrics of 'Bitchin' Camaro'. So far it was a little strained, but I did appreciate the effort. I called out, "Anybody want to play Frisbee!?"

I don't think Taz actually got airborne, but I sure wouldn't want to have to testify about it. He said, "Sir, have you brought the small human to be educated in the ways of Frisbee?"

"I have, Taz. Would you do the honors?"

"It would be my great pleasure, sir."

He went from English butler to cartoon maniac instantly. "Taz like small human, huh, huh."

Leelee kept it together until he panted at the end. Then she giggled. "You're silly, Taz!"

Taz patiently explained how to throw and catch the Frisbee. Leelee's first efforts rapidly gave way to a decent skill level, for her age. Having so many people, we started three circles. I wound up with Genny and Topper. Between Topper and I, Genny caught on quickly. Topper asked, "Sir, you may have noticed we were having difficulties with our song when you came in. Do you have any suggestions?"

"It sounded like you were trying about every variation on the lyrics that you could come up with, and nothing quite fit. Since you're playing the music anyway, couldn't you just drop out enough of the instrumental part to make it fit your lyrics?"
Topper froze a second, and Genny's throw bounced off his chest. "Sir! I think we can make that work! Thank you sir!"
Suddenly we had three fewer Frisbee players, and the shop was filled with strains of 'Bitchin' Chevelle'.
Joanna said, "I hate to break up the party, but I need to get to work."
Turning to Lyla, "Will you be here when I get back?"
"I'll be here tomorrow and the next day, at least. You don't think I'd miss out on paintball, do you?"
"Cool, see you tonight."
Topper sent me a text at that point. I wouldn't have thought he could hear over the band, but apparently he could. It read, "Sir, what is paintball?"
I sent back, "I'll get you some equipment. Don't worry, we won't leave you out."
I looked at John, "The boys want to play paintball.", in my best Igor, "I've created a monster!"
He said, "Can they really be that much worse than Dingus?"
Genny came up to me and said, "You folks really have been wonderful to us, but we need to get back to where we were headed."
"Fly careful. Watch out for whoever rigged that brooch for you."
"We'll be careful, Bob."
We all went up to the barn to say our goodbyes. Taz carried Leelee up the hill piggyback.
As they fired up and flew away, Nikki turned to me and said, "You were good with Leelee. Maybe we need to stop practicing and get serious."
"Whenever you're ready, Space Cadet."
It was getting on towards noon. I said, "I need to run in and get plates and insurance for the Chevelle. You folks want to ride along and go for lunch?"
John said, "We better go by and get Max, don't want to leave him out."
I replied, "You're right. We need to put Genny's three ounces in the safe, anyhow."
We got John and Lyla into the backseat, and Nikki took shotgun. I told everyone to buckle up, because I didn't know what to expect. I turned the key, without a thought, and she fired right up. A question came into my mind, and I rolled down my window. "Topper, where did you get gasoline?"

"Your truck still has half a tank, sir, no worries."

I looked at Ozzie. He said, "Burn 'em off, sir!"

I goosed it, and dropped the clutch. Keeping it straight wasn't bad at all, and we laid rubber all the way to the door. I was glad I bought the good suspension.

John said, "Think you used enough dynamite there, Butch?"

"Some is good, lots is gooder, and too much is just enough!"

"Your grey hair is showing, Bob."

John got out at his place, to grab the Wagoneer and Max. Snitz stayed with us, since he had his head out the window cruising the doggie internet.

We got it inspected. It wouldn't have taken so long, but they had to send out for more drool buckets.

The insurance agent wanted our firstborn, but we got him to settle for a ridiculous amount of spendolium.

Apparently, a perfect 180 into your parking spot doesn't get you a better place in line at the license office. Who knew? The ladies there are all angels. Anyway they were up in the air harpin' about something. They finally settled down and sold me some plates. One of them must have felt we were having too much fun, Jack was waiting for us when we came out.

"Bob, I can't have you enjoying this car inside city limits, I don't care how fast your reflexes are now. Besides, if you pile it up before Dee gets a crack at it, your ass is grass."

"You're right, Jack. I shouldn't have done that. Is it all the points off my license?"

"I have to look serious in front of those biddys from the office, Bob. If you crack me up, I WILL run you in."

"Did you get Sunday off?"

"I'll be there. I'm going to have to write you a warning, to make this look good."

"No problem. I deserve it."

John and Max had beaten us to the restaurant. They were standing out front with Julie and Joanna. Joanna looked like she had seen a ghost. She touched the fender, like she was trying to convince herself it was real.

She said, "It's even prettier than the first one. How did you get all the details right?"

"Nikki found an article in 'Car Craft'", I said.

"Oh shit! You mean you didn't put in the secret compartments and stuff?"

"Noo, we didn't. Do you know where they go?"

"Some of them, but I think there were one or two she never showed me."

"Bummer. I'll have to have you draw out what you remember when you get home."

We all had a nice lunch, and Snitz enjoyed his doggie bag. John and Max headed out, and we went to the sporting goods store to pick up paintball guns for the boys. Nikki said, "Should we pick up a couple more outfits in case Sergeant Mike and his friend show up?"

"Probably should. I thought they could use the gear Dingus and Dee used, but sure as I count on that, Dee will decide to come home. If we buy more gear, I'll have a few more days to square away the Chevelle."

"You really do believe in Murphy, don't you?"

"Doesn't pay not to.."

On our way home, I asked Nikki, "What do we have in the way of sneaky little spy bots?"

"We have a few pretty small bots, what are you thinking, sneaky Caveman?"

"I want to have a bot go through Dee's old car, and find all the secret compartments and cool gadgets she has hidden in it."

"Bob, we could do it that way, but."

"I'm being stupid again?"

"Caveman, I don't think you could be stupid, even if you were too drunk to fish. You're just not used to how we do things in the modern world."

"So how would you do it?"

"The one thing those grad students spent on, was a good sensor suite for that piece of junk I flew in. Three good scans from three different points, and I can tell you how old the bubblegum wrappers under the seat are."

"So we stealth up, go scan it, and turn the boys loose on mods? Easy as that?"

"Not everything has to be difficult. With our quiet mod, we won't even freak the dogs out. We could go now."

"We need to drop off the paintball stuff at John's anyhow. You mind if we take a couple of stunners, just in case?"

"Murphy loves us, and wants us to be stronger."

"You're changing, Space Cadet. It's like somebody is slowly influencing you to a new way of thinking."

"Wonder who that could be, Caveman?"

"Dee?"

I'm glad I was driving, as that kept me from the worst of the tickling.

We dropped off the paintball gear at John's, and asked Max if he would watch Snitz while we went for a flight. He was glad to. Lyla decided to stay there while we went off spying. Nikki grabbed a couple of stunners out of the closet on the way out, and we got aboard her saucer. I said, "Could you stop for a minute, while I get the door?"

"No problem."

Turns out it was a problem, for me, at least. Seems Nikki was feeling ornery, and she backed up the saucer every time I tried to get aboard. I finally remembered I had gotten better speed and reflexes when I was in the autodoc. I took a flying leap, and made it through the door. Nikki was laughing so hard, tickling her at that point wouldn't have done a thing. I shut the door, shaking my head at how much my life had changed. When she started moving air again, she messed with something on the control panel. She finished, and said, "There, it's sent out. Grandpa and Dee will get a kick out of that!"

"Your day will come, Space Cadet."

"Ooh, scary Caveman!"

We arrived over the Chevelle, and Nikki set the autopilot to hold position. Then she started the scan. I asked, "How long does it take?"

"Two minutes for each axis, and we need all three to make a good picture. Stealth is functioning at full capacity, we should be able to get what we need."

Top and side went smooth, but the car was too close to the house to get the saucer between them. That left us bending over a patch of weeds in front of the car. Just our luck, the guy looked out the kitchen window about halfway through the scan. I asked, "Is this thing bulletproof?"

"Yes, but if he gets an emitter, we may have fun getting back."

"Can you rotate while it's scanning?"

"Nope. Get a stunner and get ready by the door. I'll give you a firing angle as soon as I can."

I got low, figuring he would aim at the middle of the door. I heard a sound like hail, and then the scan finished. The saucer turned, and the door began to slide open. As soon as I had a gap to shoot through, I stunned him. Repeatedly. Until the door shut. Nikki said, "He's down, Caveman. Ease up."

"You're a fine one to talk, after you emptied your power pack in that punk the other day."

"Okay, you're right, but I was a little emotional. I thought he killed my brand new Caveman."

"Did we at least get a good scan?"

"Oh yeah. This puny computer will take a little bit to crunch it all, but we have the data."

"Next question. Do we have enough computer to compare two scans and tell us what's different?"

"We do. You want to scan the new car and see what's not the same?"

"I do. Be easier than trying to find everything ourselves. Dee probably hid things well."

"We can do that. Of course, your modernizations will show up too. Those you'll have to pick out yourself."

"Good enough. I should probably see if Jack is working today, he could help talk that guy out of his UFO story."

I dialed Jack. "Officer Conway, how may I help you today?"

"Jack, you may get a call about some turkey shooting at a UFO in his back yard. Any chance you could talk him down?"

"Mrs. Watson, It's usually the Fire Department that gets cats out of trees, but if I'm out that way, I'll stop by."

"Thanks, Jack. See you Sunday."

"And a fine day to you as well, Mrs. Watson."

"First I'm the dry cleaner, and now I'm a little old lady with a cat up a tree. Gotta get a better system for the phones."

"What are you muttering about, Caveman?"

"The BS stories people come up with to play off talking to me on the phone. Makes me sound like their drug connection, or something."

"We're here. You might want to call and tell John we're scanning."

I dialed again. "Hey, John, If you fail to see something in the driveway, that's us. We're scanning the new car to compare to the old one."

"Yesterday, upon the stair, I met a man who wasn't there?"

"Exactly."

"Is Nikki going to let you out of the saucer?"

"You saw that, eh?"

"We did. Live it down, you will not, young Padawan."

"You want a pup?"

"Payback finally deliver?"

"She's fixing to."

"Big words, Bob, big words."

"See you in a few."

When the scans finished, Nikki flew over to the barn, and paused so I could get out and open the door. Just to be sure, I jumped clear of the saucer, rather than climbing down. Once she parked, I went to meet her, but it took her longer than I would have expected. Investigating, I found her working with the ship's computer. She looked up. "Hi, Caveman. Remembered I could network the saucers' computers and get the data crunched faster."

"Oh, you're crapping on them, I see."

"I'm not defecating, what are you talking about?"

"In the old Unix days, there was a program to let you use free time on other computers on your network. It was called crp. To invoke it, you typed crp on. Since it slowed down the other computers, it became known as 'crapping on' them."

"Crp becomes crap, because cavemen's favorite hobby is to make things sound nasty, I see now, Caveman. Anyway, I'm done. Let's go in the house while this runs."

John said, "Jack called and asked if I had to pluck birdshot out of your ass. I don't, do I?"

"Nope, he only caught the saucer. By the time he had a shot at me, he was already stunned."

"How many times did you hit him? Jack said he was slow coming around."

"Not as many as Nikki did that punk the other day. She shut the door on me, party pooper!"

John took the stunner I was carrying and ran back the firing log. "You had yours on maximum, hers was only on standard."

"She drained her pack."

"Her pack was already partially drained. Yours was full. You really don't like this guy, do you?"

"It was bad enough when I just had a mental picture of what that car was like in its prime. Now that I've driven the new one, letting the old one rust is even worse."

"You said yourself, getting it away from him wouldn't be worth the effort."

"I know. Doesn't make me like it. Did Jack have a lot of trouble with that guy?"

"He said that once he explained that if he took his UFO report, he'd have to take notice of the fact the fella had discharged a firearm in city limits, in an unsafe manner, while drunk, and on probation, the fellow wasn't interested in filing a report any more."

"That's good, at least. If it had taken him another minute to walk by that window, we would have been gone. Bad luck."

"Why did you stun him?"

"If he had managed to take out one of our stealth emitters, we would have been in a bad way. Figured the exposure was less this way."
"Probably right, but it's still more exposure than we need."
"I know. Dee's car is turning into quite the project."
Nikki's comm chimed. "Snagfart!! It's worse than you thought, Caveman. There's a piece of Galactic tech hidden in that car. Must be something her Grandpa gave her."
John said, "Can you tell what it is?"
"No, its power is too far gone for that. We need to retrieve it. Tech like that in the hands of someone not rated acceptable contact is a big breach."
"He doesn't know he has it, does he?", John asked.
I said, "He knows he has something. He wanted a hundred grand for the car, and looked like he wanted to shoot me when that didn't totally run me off."
Nikki said, "This is hidden really well, and it has a lock besides. It will take a little time to retrieve it. No way we can count on him not to notice us."
I replied, "If he hasn't found it yet, he's not going to in the next few days."
"Hey, weren't you going to call the lawyer today?"
I called the lawyer, and got him started on finding out about buying Shady Oaks. He told me he couldn't get much done this afternoon, it would be the first of the week before he had much, but he would call when he did. I offered him a ten percent commission on the deal, going down a half percent a day starting Tuesday. He seemed more interested, and I said I looked forward to hearing from him. John said, "You just destroyed his weekend, you know that, right?"
"Ten percent on what has to be a several million dollar deal? I think he'll get over it."
Nikki asked, "You guys want to come over for supper? I bet I can talk Caveman into grilling."
John said, "Sounds good, but you know we're going to have to find him enough time to do his famous chili sometime soon. I got the Jones."
Nikki fiddled with her watch. "It's too late in the day for him to feed your chili addiction, John. We'll see about tomorrow."
"Guess I'll have to settle for roasted animal parts."
I said, "You, too, John?"
Max interjected, "Can I get some of those roasted animal parts?"
Lyla purred, "Roasted animal parts! Mmm, mmm."

Defeated, I said, "I think I'll go see if I can fail to get in the Chevelle. Everybody got their cameras on?"

I took shotgun, but I didn't hand Nikki the keys 'til Lyla and Snitz had gotten in. "It has Ginormous power, with a capital G. Go easy."

"No sideways?"

"You want to tell the boys they have to start from scratch?"

"No sideways!"

Nikki went around back to the shop. I called the boys to run the door up. Topper asked me as soon as we stopped, "Is it acceptable, sir?"

"Acceptable! Oh hell no, it is not just acceptable! It's fabulous, fantastic, freaking amazing!"

Ozzie asked, "Did you drive it hard, sir?"

"We did. It did all we could ask and more. You boys are artistes."

Taz said, a little dejected, "So the project is over? Do you have more work for us?"

"Well, Taz, I made a mistake. I didn't learn enough about the car we were copying before I started you fellas on this. There are some extra features that need to be added."

Ozzie looked maniacal. "More power, sir!?"

"No, Ozzie, she's got plenty of power. Dee had secret compartments in hers. Once we get the scans processed, I'll send them to you, and you can tell me what you need to make the modifications."

Taz said, "Secret compartments!? James frikkin' Bond? COOL!"

Nikki's comm beeped. She said, "Here we go. Topper, if I send you the file, can you display it?"

"Of course ma'am. If I might ask, is the paintwork satisfactory, as well?"

I said, "Sorry, Topper, I got carried away. Someone who had seen the original car told us this one was even more beautiful. Sadly, she is also the one who told us we had forgotten to put in the secret compartments."

Topper mused, "More beautiful, you say, sir?"

"That is what she said."

Topper gave us a life sized hologram of the car, with differences highlighted in red. All three bots froze for a minute, networked and studying the scans. The hologram changed, showing some changes still in red, the things we had improved in green, and a few they weren't sure about in yellow. I asked, "Topper, can you enlarge each yellow change in order, so we can decide how to class them?"

"Certainly sir. None of these changes will affect the paint. I am relieved."

"It would be a tragedy to ruin your beautiful paint, Topper."

We went through all the yellows, the reds, and then we went through the greens just to be sure. I told the boys not to worry about the items actually hidden in the compartments, I would deal with those. The boys communed again, and texted me a shopping list. I told them I would go to town tomorrow, and they should do what they could with what they had on hand. Suddenly, Lyla, who had been fascinated with all the custom tweaks on the car, said, "Hey, wait a minute, where's my saucer?"

Topper said, "A space opened up in the barn. We assumed you would want it closer to the house. We also took the liberty of bringing your training machine up to Mr. Wilson's standards. We can move it back, if you want."

"No, that's fine. I was just surprised. What was that about the training machine?"

"You're not aware of Mr. and Mrs. Wilson's recent improvements? They found and eliminated the source of training headache."

Lyla turned to Nikki and I. "What's he talking about? The machine gives the shots, now?"

Nikki said, "We found what was causing the headache in the first place, well, Snitz did, and we fixed it. No more shots."

"That's wonderful! Can I write a story about that?"

I spoke up, "I suppose, but it's not that big a thing. We just had a dog to show us where to look."

Lyla said, "What was Dee saying about capes?"

I said, "I think it's time to start the fire."

John and Max showed up a little later. I asked John, "Do you have any ideas for how to retrieve that tech stashed in Dee's old car?"

"We could hire somebody to put him in the hospital, and get it while he's not there."

"Gee, if he's gonna get hurt, I don't wanna farm it out, but I was hoping we could avoid having that much fun. We are still trying to keep a low profile, you know."

"You want to hire somebody to follow him around, tell us when he's not home?"

"I'm not convinced he doesn't have some kind of alarm. It was awfully convenient, him looking out right when he did."

"This is just so screwy. He knows there's something about that car that's special, but he has no clue what. He doesn't try to lock it up, just leaves it in the yard. It's almost like he's trying to get someone to come after it."

"Not only does he not know what's special about the car, he hasn't even tried to find it. Dee's hidey holes are still stocked. Even the easy one under the dash that just takes a tap to open. If he was as hard up for cash as he looks, he would have at least sold her guns."

"Guns, plural?"

"That one under the dash holds a sweet little 38 snubbie. The driver's side taillight is on a hinge like a 57 Chevy. There's a Remington 870 up over the back tire. I can send you the file if you want to see all of them."

"There's more? Have to wonder what Dee was into, back in the day."

"That you do. More to our Dee than meets the eye, and that's sayin' something."

"Ain't it though. Dingus is gonna have to go back in the box, just to rest up."

"You wanna go to the range in the morning? I need to see how many of her hiding places I can restock. The boys think they can have everything set up by Sunday."

"You're expecting them for paintball, aren't you?"

"Rather be ready than not. You hear anything from Mike?"

"Haven't yet. The Major is probably watching him like a hawk."

The food was ready to come off the grill, so we took it inside. Nikki and Lyla had a surprise. They had made rolls to go with everything else. We had a good meal, and it was a nice evening, so we all wandered out and played Frisbee with Snitz. When it began to get dark, John said, "I think it's about time for Max and I to head home. See you in the morning, Bob?"

"Yep. Hey, why don't you sic that hacker you used, on our friend with the shotgun. Maybe we could learn something."

"Good idea. See you tomorrow."

Joanna made it home not too long after that. After she got a shower, I sat down at the kitchen table with her. "You don't need to worry about drawing those hiding spots, we got a scan of the old car this afternoon. I gotta ask, though, why so many guns?"

"Her husband, Bill, didn't let her keep any in the house. Said it wasn't ladylike. She got in the habit of keeping everything important in the car. She doesn't have more firepower in that car than you do in your safe, does she, Bob?"

"No, I don't suppose she does. When her son took her car, he disarmed her, too, all in one fell swoop?"

"He did. Cackled about it. Nasty piece of work, he is."

"How did Dee wind up with a no account son?"

"He's adopted, and Bill wasn't much for discipline."

"Hopefully she won't have to deal with him any more."

"Have you been able to get that trinket her Grandpa gave her? You've done a heck of a job on the car, but I think that meant as much as it did."

"If it's what I think it is, we know where it is, but we haven't figured out how to get it back yet."

"It's still in the car?"

"Yep. The guy who has it is squirrelly as 40 acres of oaks, or I would have bought it already."

"Carl Jackson?"

"You know him?"

"Young William's go to man for dirty deeds."

"Keeps coming back to William. I had hoped not to have to deal with him."

"First person I heard say that was his first grade teacher."

"Doesn't sound like we'll solve it tonight then."

Nikki came in, asking "You two about done? Some of us need rest."

"Sure, Space Cadet, just finishing up. Where is everyone sleeping?"

"Lyla says it's time we had our bed back. She's sleeping in her saucer, since the boys brought it up to the barn. She said you're welcome to join her, Joanna."

"I get to sleep in a flying saucer? This beats Shitty Oaks all to pieces!"

"Shitty Oaks?", I asked.

"It's what the inmates, oops, I mean patients, call Shady Oaks when the nurses can't hear."

"We should be able to fix that. Got a man working on it."

"What color cape did you want, Bob?"

"You say you're short of tickles, Joanna?"

"Save those for your wife, Bobby Apples."

"Ow! Haven't heard that in thirty years, at least. Good Night!"

Later, Nikki asked, "Bobby Apples? What was that about?"

"It was a name some of the other kids called me. Not my favorite."

Snitz was certain, that even though it was Saturday, it was still very important to check the outdoors promptly at sunrise. I started coffee on the way out. We wandered down to see how things were going at the shop. Topper greeted us. "Hello sir, I was about to text you, we have accomplished all we can without more supplies. I do have a question, however."

"What's that?"

"The one small compartment that locks. On the old car, it would open with the trunk key. The new one should open with the trunk key for this car, correct?"

"Yes, that would be best. Once you have your supplies, how long will it take to finish up?"

"If we get what we need by noon today, we should have it ready by sunrise, if the maintenance bots are not needed elsewhere."

"I'll get you what you need as soon as I can. You guys are great! Thanks for all your hard work."

Taz asked, "You will have more work for us after this, won't you sir?"

"Of course, Taz, I'll keep you fellas busy. Why are you worried?"

"If you don't need us any more, you might sell us to someone who doesn't treat us as well. We wouldn't be able to play music, or Frisbee."

"You guys can stay as long as you like, even if I do run out of things for you to do. You don't need to worry. I won't sell you."

In chorus, the boys said, "Thank you, sir!"

"About this sir stuff, do you think you could call me boss, instead?"

"Sure, Boss."

By the time we made it back to the house, all three ladies were sitting at the table with coffee. I got a cup, and started breakfast. Nikki started fiddling with her watch, looked up and said, "Bob, dear, are you set on buying all new guns for Dee?"

"Bob, dear. I must have really been a moron this time. Hit me, Nikki, whatcha got?"

"Well, truth be told, I was a moron first. Does that help?"

"We both need to do better? When are the grown ups supposed to be back, anyway?"

"I haven't heard, Caveman. You know those folks who left all those saucers for us to salvage?"

"Yes, Patrol or pirates?"

"Pirates. What do they do for a living?"

"Uhh, stop ships and take stuff?"

"Yes. How do you suppose they do that without getting shot all the time?"

"Enlighten me, Professor."

"They rig a boarding craft with a big stunner, that can knock people down on a neighboring ship."

"Okay. I don't get... Oh! A house would pass stunner beams at least as good as a saucer. We could have stunned that idiot and avoided all the drama."

"How long do you think it would take the boys to clean out all the secret compartments?"

"With all their little helpers? Not over a minute, I would think."

"Let's wait 'til dark this time."

"Sounds like a plan, but let's see what John has to say."

I called John and put him on speaker. "Morning John, you're on with all of us. Nikki has a plan. I'd like to run it by you before we run off half cocked again."

"Okay, shoot."

Nikki said, "We have a boarding saucer the pirates rigged up. It has a big stunner that could knock that turkey out inside his house. Bob says the boys can clean out the secret compartments in about a minute. I want to go get all of Dee's stuff tonight."

"You didn't use the big stunner yesterday because?"

"I didn't even remember we had it. I was just focused on the good scanner we needed to find everything."

"We need to start planning things out better, or our secret is going to get out."

"Agreed. Do you see anything wrong with this plan?"

"What can stop a stunner beam? Do you have a scanner that can tell if he's stunned or just asleep?"

"This stunner is designed to go through a saucer hull, so even a metal roof shouldn't be a problem. We can definitely scan him before we move to the retrieval part of the plan, however."

"Sounds good enough. When do you plan on executing it?"

"After dark, say three a.m., so most people are asleep."

"You turkeys are learning, slowly. I guess this means our range trip is off, Bob?"

"You could ride along while I gather Topper's shopping list, if you want."

"Sounds good."

"I'll be over in a little bit."

I picked up John and we headed in. He said, "Bob, I've been thinking."

"I thought I smelled smoke."

"You've got very little in the way of medical knowledge, right?"

"That's true. I know almost enough to hand you the right thing the first time."

"I was thinking it would make a lot more sense for me to buy Shady Oaks, rather than you."

"Would you please? I'm getting in over my head. I didn't want to take it on, but I couldn't let Joanna down."

"You could ask for help, Bob. We all just think, 'Oh, Bob can fix that', never think, 'damn, Bob's busy already, maybe I should take this one'."

"At least Nikki has started calling me out when I'm about to screw up and do things the hard way."

"Have I mentioned she's good for you?"

"Think you might of. Hey, can you think of anything else we can do to make sure things go slick tonight?"

"You said something about thinking he had an alarm. A motion detector would pick up a saucer even if it was cloaked, wouldn't it?"

"Snagfart, Yes! Why didn't I think about that. I've got to pop my head out before I get us caught."

"Easy, Bob. We're all new at this. I bet he has it hooked to a camera."

"We don't want the boys on Youtube, do we?"

"No, we do not, unless it's the band."

"We should have scanned the house first."

"Probably. How can we take out a camera?"

"Let me ask."

I called Nikki. "Space Cadet, John and I are having a little discussion. What do we have that will take out a video camera?"

"A regular Earth standard surveillance camera?"

"Yes."

"A stunner puts out enough voltage to fry the chips in one of those, Caveman."

"Next question. Could you please get into Carl's computer, and erase any video he got of us yesterday, and trace down where he might have sent it, and do likewise?"

"I could, but it would be quicker and easier to net the saucers up again and let them do it."

"Whatever you think best, Space Cadet. Just remember we're trying to keep a low profile, okay? If you have to yank it back from Youtube, make it look like they took it down for some kind of violation, instead of it vanishing in a puff of logic."

"Gotcha, Caveman."

"Thanks, Sweetheart. Talk to you later."

"Bye."

"That work, John?'

"Sounds right. You want another shooter, in case he has more than one camera?"

"You're more than welcome, as long as the boys have room to work. Reminds me, I should let them know what's going on."

I called Topper. Strains of 'Bitchin' Chevelle' faded out as he answered. "Boss, what can three out of work robots do for you today?"

"Well, Topper, I need you to come up with a plan. We're going to clean out all the secret compartments on the old car tonight. I need you and the boys to come up with the quickest way for you three and the maintenance bots to clear them all out, and close them again. You will have to make keys, in case the car is locked, and one for the locked compartment. Any questions?"

"We get to go on a caper? You're the best boss ever! We'll be ready."

"We want to strike about three in the morning, to avoid attention. We should be back with your parts in an hour or so. Can you plan your work so you'll be able to down tools about 2:30?"

"No problem, Boss."

"See you shortly, then. Bye."

"Goodbye, Boss."

We gathered up Topper's list. Some of the springs and hinges he wanted were hard to find. We got as close as we could, and hoped he could make do. I figured most of what was on Dee's original were junkyard parts, off of who knows what. We stopped off at the range, so I could stock up on cleaning supplies and get fresh ammo for Dee's guns. When I backed into the shop, my truck was swarmed by bots looking for material to finish their jobs. We stayed in the truck, out of the way, until the rush ended. We finished unloading what the piranhas had left, and put the gun supplies on a bench over by where my safes were sitting. I needed to get those put in the house, soon. I took John back to his place, and we called the lawyer to let him know to put John's name on the paperwork, not mine. He hadn't started drawing up papers yet, so we caught him soon enough. My comm rang soon after we got off the phone. "Bob Wilson, how may I help you?"

I recognized Mike's voice. "Yes, I was wondering if I would be able to pick up my dry cleaning tomorrow? What time will you be open?"

"Paintball usually starts about one in the afternoon. You might want to get in a little early to get familiar with the rules and equipment, since you haven't played before."

"I see. Ensign Whittum asked me to inquire if her dry cleaning was also ready for pickup?"

"Bring her along, the more, the merrier."
"Very good. I'll bring her ticket when I come to pick up mine."
He disconnected. I said to John, "We've really got to come up with a better method for secure comm. I'm tired of being his dry cleaner."
"He's fooling the Major with that crap?"
"I doubt it. Probably giving the Major plausible denial. My guess would be the Major's sister is all up in his stuff about Bill, so that he has to come down on us to keep her happy, but he would rather have us here than not. If he really wanted us gone, we'd be gone."
"That makes sense, but it kinda leaves us hanging by a thread of the Major's good will, doesn't it?"
"We're sneaking around working with alien tech our own government would gladly kill us to get ahold of, when was this outfit ever anything but precarious?"
"You're right, Orville."
"Aah, Wilbur!"
"Need more peanut butter there, Ed."
"I'm just horsing around."
"You guys want to come to Chez John to dine this evening?"
"Sounds good to me, I'll run it by the management when I get back."
I drove home, of course Snitz was waiting to scold me for going driving without him. Gotta keep up with that doggie internet, don't you know. I found a Frisbee, and we played for a while. Joanna left for work, then Lyla and Nikki came out to play. Nikki asked, "So how did it go? Get everything the boys needed?"
"I'm convinced some of the parts on the old car are junkyard scrounge, no telling what make and model they're off of. We got as close as we could, without taking all day. John wants us to come over for supper. Is that okay with you two?"
Lyla spoke up, "Sounds good!"
Nikki said, "I'd like that."
"Reminds me, I need to start a pot of chili for tomorrow before I go to bed tonight."
Lyla said, "Chili and paintball? I'm glad I stayed."
I pulled out my phone and called John. A Frisbee bounced off my head when I looked at the phone to dial. Snitz grabbed it and ran it back before I could retaliate. "Hi, John, we'll be there for supper."
"Good."
"I need to hang up, I'm a Frisbee target. Bye."

"Bye, Bob."

We had some lunch, and I decided to grab a nap, since it looked like a busy night. As I headed out to the saucer, Nikki decided that was a good idea. So much for sleeping.

We got cleaned up, and loaded up to head to John's. I made sure to grab some Frisbees. Snitz and I rode in the back of the truck, since Joanna had Nikki's rig. Snitz had a great time. Doggie broadband!

I found Max when we arrived, and asked, "You've got a good inventory of what we have on hand, correct?"

"I do, Bob. What do you need?"

"That's just it, Max. I don't have a clue! Could you maybe build me a report of what we have on hand, and what it can be used for, maybe broken into categories like construction, vehicle repair, weapons, and so forth? Nikki has to keep telling me about things we have that we can use to fix problems. I'd like to be able to study up and get some idea of what we actually have on hand, and what it's good for."

"I've got a pretty good tally of everything, broken into categories, like you said, but I'll have to add descriptions for what you want. Give me a minute, I think I can write a script to take care of it while we eat, and I can give it to you before you leave. That work?"

"That's great! Thanks, Max!"

I found John out by the grill. "So, partner, how many problems do you have with tonight's op?"

"I'm scared, Bob. I can't figure any way to do it better than we already are. I know we're missing something, but I don't know what."

"I know what you mean. I come up with a plan and then Nikki says, 'Oh, Bob, don't be silly, do it like this'. I wish I had a good enough idea of what Galactic tech can do to make good plans. I'm sure somewhere in my barn, there's a magic doohickey that makes tonight's raid child's play, but I don't even know it exists."

"Maybe if we figure out the kind of thing that would make it easier, we could ask Nikki if it exists."

"Might work, but first you better turn those steaks."

"Thanks. I got distracted. In all the UFO movies, they have that thing that stops all the electronics. I wonder if that's real. Would beat the heck out of overloading his cameras with a stunner and leaving physical evidence."

"Good idea. The little flashy thing to make him forget would be handy, too."

"Judging by what we've seen, they can probably do it, but it will take twenty minutes under a headset, and leave him a nasty headache."

"Sounds right. Don't think we want to go to all that trouble tonight."

"Am I the only one that will be glad when Dingus gets back to show us the error in our ways?"

"Not at all. I feel so much better when we have adult supervision, Bob."

"You think they'll show up for paintball?"

"Wouldn't bet against it, but I'm not sure. It's a big galaxy, Dee's probably got a lot of things she wants to see."

"Those steaks are about right. Time to feed some people."

While we ate, I asked Nikki about shutting down the electronics remotely, without lasting damage. She thought a minute, and said, "I don't know how to do that, Bob."

Max tinkered with his watch a minute, and said, "I see why you want that inventory, Bob. The saucer you're going to use tonight has that capability too, to keep it's prey from getting a message off or running. I'll send you both the file on how it works."

"Is it a wide area thing, or will we be able to just target his house?"

"His neighbors will probably get hit, too. You're not going to be there very long, are you?"

"Nope. We want to be gone before anyone notices we are there. John, is there any way to find out if anyone around him is on critical medical equipment? I don't want to kill anybody over a few guns and a keepsake, even if it is Galactic."

John said, "The ambulance district has a database of people with medical devices. Nikki, do you think you can get in and out without leaving digital traces?"

"Is a bear Catholic? Does the Pope shit in the woods? You really want to get sniped tomorrow, don't you, John?"

"Sorry for offending your High and Mightyness, oh great and powerful Oz, I mean, Nikki."

Lyla said, "That's the lamest apology I've ever heard."

Nikki replied, "That's 'cause he's not sorry, yet!"

John showed her the website for District, and she was into the list quickly. She fiddled with something else, and then said, "The nearest house we would need to be concerned about is over a mile away. Unless that jammer has monster output, it should be safe."

I said, "One less thing to worry about. So, the plan is, hit him with the big stunner, scan to make sure he's down, and then turn on the jammer?"

Nikki replied, "I think so, yes."

"Will the jammer affect our bots?"

Max searched his inventory. "All of the maintenance and cargo bots are hardened against the kind of field it puts out. I think the pirates used them to clean out captured ships."

"This sounds like it's coming together. Is it just using advanced tech to pull it off that's making it seem easy, or are we missing something big?"

John said, "I'm with you, Bob. It seems too easy, but I don't know what other precautions we can take at this point."

"If anyone has a suggestion, now would be the time."

Nikki said, "I could program a recall order for the bots and an escape flight, all on a panic button."

"Please do. Anything else?"

No one had any more suggestions. Max's script finished, and he sent me the inventory with training wheels.

I asked John, "You still want to ride along?"

"I do. I want to see all this go down."

"The saucer we need is in your barn. Did you learn to fly, yet?"

"I did. Want me to bring it when I come?"

"That would be great. Meet us at the new shop, about 2:30."

"I'll be there."

Lyla, Nikki, and I went back to our place, but Snitz stayed with Max. Taking him on a raid where we were using tech we hadn't tried yet seemed like a bad idea. Joanna pulled in not long after we got back. She got cleaned up, then she and Lyla headed out to the saucer so we could rest a few hours before we needed to be up again.

The alarm went off way too soon. I went and started the coffee I set up before we laid down, then I went back to wake Nikki and get dressed. As we were walking down to the shop, I heard the door go up, and then the sound of whistling. I looked at Nikki and said, "We better hurry, they'll leave without us."

"John might, but the boys won't go without their Boss."

We hurried to get aboard. John turned over the piloting duties to Nikki, and she set up her panic button before we started out. John handed me a stunner, and we waited by the door. Topper said, "Thank you for including us, Boss."

"We need your crew to be able to get in and out quickly. If anyone has problems with the jammer, put them back aboard, and we'll improvise. How is the car coming?"

"We should be able to have it ready by sunup, if we don't take too long doing this."

"Sunup is plenty of time. If it wasn't done 'til lunch, it wouldn't be a problem."

"Have we mentioned how much we like working for you, Boss?"

"You might have said something, I suppose."

Nikki called out, "Cut the chatter! We're over the target. Delivering stun now. Scan shows him down. Let's get this done before he wakes up. Electronics are down, ready by the door." John and I got out of the bots way.

Nikki said, "Go!" as the door opened. John and I kept a watch for nosy neighbors. Bots started filing back aboard with whatever they found in their assigned compartment. Topper stood outside the door to help the smaller bots on the saucer. Taz was inside, counting the returning bots, and Ozzie was receiving the items and stowing them as the bots came aboard. Taz said, "All of us are aboard, Topper. Let's go!"

Topper grasped the edges of the doorway and pulled himself aboard. He said, "We may depart, Ma'am."

The door was closing before he finished saying depart. I could see the ground receding as the door closed. Nikki called, "Jammer off. Returning home. Anyone have a problem?"

One of the small bots, holding a key, and a small device, chittered at Topper. He said, "It wants to know if it should begin charging the device, Boss?"

"Let's wait until we know what it is, Topper. We don't need surprises."

"Yes, Boss."

Nikki ran the door of the shop up. She landed and opened the door. Topper asked, "What should we do with the recovered items, Boss?"

"Put them on the bench where I left the gun cleaning supplies, Topper."

It was a joy to see the boys practicing safe weapon handling. After they had put all the loot on the table, they went back to working on the Chevelle. John, Nikki, and I went over to the table to see what all we had retrieved. John and I started clearing weapons, and Nikki picked up the Galactic tech. She said, "I'm not sure what this is, I'll have to research it."

"Good thing we didn't let them charge it, then."

After the weapons were safe, we started looking at the other items. We found a large roll of cash, some silver ounces, a couple of Krugerrands, and some documents. She also had a few nice knives and some safe deposit box keys. John was looking over her weapons. "Colt Detective Special, good thing you decided to clean out the old car, you would have had a heck of a time finding another one of those."

"Walther PPK, pre-war, commercial, in 32, that wouldn't have been a picnic, either, John. I'll have to clean these in the morning. It's bedtime."

Topper asked, "Do you want us to put things back in their places, when we finish modifying the car, Boss?"

"Please leave that until I've had a better chance to examine everything, Topper."

John got aboard, and took the saucer back to his barn. Nikki ran the door down, and we headed off to bed. Snitz wasn't there to get me up, so my comm went off instead. "Bob Wilson, it better be good, this early in the morning."

"Shake your lazy tail, son. Come out and open the barn for us."

Sure enough, Dingus and Dee were back. "On my way, Dingus."

I hung up and found my jeans. I stumbled out and went to open the barn doors. I got goosed by the rim of a saucer. "Oh, crap! He let Dee drive home." She backed off and let me pull the doors open. She set it down in one of our last free spaces. We either need to sell some saucers, or build more parking. Dingus walked out, and I shook his hand. "Good to have you back, Dingus. We could use some adult supervision around here."

"Well, you're out of luck then. Dee's got me feeling like a kid again."

"I bet she does. You teach her that trick with the edge of the saucer?"

"Nope. She figured that one out herself. Been practicing so she could tap you just right."

"So the Galactics made you bring her home, to keep them safe from her?"

"They just didn't want to have to play poker with her anymore."

"I'd believe that. Come on in the house, we'll get some breakfast going. What's keeping Dee?"

"She'll be along. She knows where the house is, don't worry."

After we were out of earshot, I said, "I need your help with some stuff after breakfast, if you don't mind."

"What kind of stuff?"

"Surprise for Dee."

"You know I need to be in on that."

I got coffee going, and put some bacon in the oven. Dingus started pancakes, and cracked eggs to scramble. Dingus asked, "How many this morning?"

"Six. Lyla and Joanna are sleeping in Lyla's saucer."

"Joanna?"

"Friend of Dee's from Shitty Oaks."

"Any way we could do something about that place?'

"They're fixing to have a change in management. That ought to help."

"Oh?"

"John's buying the place."

"You boys are alright, Bob. You figure to do more recruiting out of there?"

"Depends on if Dee thinks anybody else is worth it, I guess."

Nikki came wandering in, eyes half open. "What are you doing up, Caveman? Snitz wasn't here to wake you up."

"We got company, Space Cadet."

"Whaa? Oh, hi Grandpa. Where's Dee?"

"In the saucer getting cleaned up. She flew all the way in."

"She likes saucers then?"

"She said it was almost as good as her old Chevelle, whatever that means."

Nikki looked around to see if Dee had snuck in. "Hang on, Grandpa, you'll probably know what that means by the end of the day."

I heard the screen door, and said, "Yeah, we've been having really pretty weather. Should be great for paintball today. I want to try out those courses you sicced me on, Dingus."

Dingus caught on quick. Nikki looked like she was going to say something, but Dee came around the corner. "Hello, sleepyhead."

A big hug later, Nikki said, "Dee, it's great to see you. Are you going to help me keep Caveman in line?"

"Space Ranger there takes all my time these days, sorry."

"Did you guys have a good time?"

"We had a lot of fun, when Dingus wasn't doing official stuff. He is kind of a big deal, it seems."

"Tell me about it. All those stories when I was growing up about 'your Grandpa Dingolus', now that I've met him, they don't smell nearly so fishy."

"He's the real deal, Sweety. But your man Bob ain't no slouch, his own self."

"I only have to smack him around a couple times a week to keep him in line, he's getting better."

"Where's that dog you were so proud of?"

"We had some stuff to do last night. Had to leave him with Dad."

"Stuff to do, huh? Still 'practicing', are you?"

"Not just that, silly. Snitz is used to that."

"So what, then?"

"You'll find out later. Let's get Lyla and Joanna up so we can eat."

Just then the screen door popped open. Lyla said, "No need, we're up. Is that Dingus' saucer in the barn?"

Dee said, "It'll be mine if I can talk him out of it."

Joanna gushed, "Delilah, it's so good to see you! Thank you for getting me out of that place!"

Dee said, "Just Dee, now. This one here took my Lilah." pointing at Lyla.

"Wha..? Oh, that would be confusing, wouldn't it?"

"Yep. Besides, Bob and his bunch got you out, I just told 'em who to grab."

"Have you heard? John is buying that place."

"Really? That's great! So instead of bingo, they're going to run Wednesday night capers? Sneak attacks on the day-old counter at the bakery?"

"I wouldn't put it past him, but I haven't heard any plans yet."

"We'll get it out of him this afternoon, after we beat him at paintball."

"Julie said we both needed to take off for that. Why is it such a big deal for this bunch?"

"They get the whole crew together and have fun. It's like family, without the genetics."

Lyla spoke up, "Speaking of family, are you and Dingus going to make it official?"

"We got a Galactic partner contract while we were gone, but we want to do a regular ceremony when we get a chance."

"Congratulations! Can I come if I don't write about it?"

"Honey, you know somebody is going to write about the 'Great Dingolus Slongum" marrying a native girl. Might as well be somebody who likes us. How 'bout an exclusive?"

"Really? If I'd known almost getting killed would be this good for my career, I would have done it years ago."

"You're not just visiting?"

"Nope. Ran out here on a crime story, and picked up a nice breaking news tale while I was here."

"Crime story? What did they catch Bob at?"

"No, silly. They rescued a little girl and her Grandma, in an out of control saucer. Turns out it was sabotage."

"What's the other one? Did Bob get a cat?"

"No, I did a story on Nikki and him fixing the teaching machines."

"The fellas at the Guide were all over that. The power core mods, too, once Dingus told them his guano story."

"We saw one of those, too. It smelled awful."

"Bob didn't fix all the saucers here? I thought he would."

"He did. The Patrol hid one of theirs in a cave while they were here."

They went on like that, all through breakfast, getting caught up. When we were through eating, I asked Dingus, "You mind helping me with a few things?"

He replied, "Not at all, Bob."

Dee asked, "Where are they off to?"

Nikki said, "Secret Bob stuff, who knows?"

As we neared the shop, Dingus asked, "What's that noise?"

I pulled out my comm and dialed Topper. "Sorry, boys. Band practice is over. Coming in with company."

Dingus wondered, "Boys? Who you got working for you?"

"You'll see. They're a hoot."

We walked in. The boys were goofing around until they saw who was with me. They lined up and stood tall. Topper said, "Major Slongum, it is a pleasure to see you again, I hope your travels were pleasant?"

"They were, ZZ809. Thank you."

"Sir, I have a new designation. I am now called Topper."

"As do I. They promoted me to colonel when I retired. Has Mr. Wilson kept you busy?"

"Yes, sir, he has provided us things to do. Not all of them productive, but he has kept us busy."

"You three have a band?"

"Well, sir, two of us are named for musical acts. When we found video of an all robot band on the internet, it seemed like a good way to spend time when we don't have a project going."

"What sorts of 'projects'?"

"This building, for example. We dug the foundation, poured the slab, and assembled the building kit the Boss had delivered. We also plumbed and wired it. Mr. Wilson is a good boss. He has taught us new work skills, and new skills for recreation."

"Recreation?"

"The Frisbee is fun. The canine enjoys it a great deal."

"You help to exercise the dog?"

"We do. We also entertained the small human, while she was here. Taz especially. I think he misses her."

"I see removing your personality locks was the right thing to do. I had worried about how you and Mr. Wilson would interact."

Taz spoke up, "He is our Boss, sir. We are very glad to be here."

Ozzie said, "He let us build the Chevelle of great power. See its trail?". He pointed to where I laid rubber leaving the shop.

"Wait a minute, I've heard that word before. What is a Chevelle?"

They parted, to give him a view of the car. Topper said, "This, sir, is a Chevelle. It is not an exact replica of the original, but we have endeavored to improve it in any way we could."

"This is Dee's horse?"

I said, "Yessir, it is. Luckily, Joanna knew more about it than I did, or we would have missed a lot of stuff. That's what I need your help with, getting things ready to go back in the new car."

"New car? So this isn't the one she built?"

"Sadly, no. That one is rusting away, in a backyard. It's owned by a crony of her son, who wouldn't sell it. We did get scans, to locate all the special features, and last night we went and retrieved all her hidden items. They are over here."

We went over to the table, and I started separating things that needed service from things that could go back as is. Topper started the small bots putting away what was ready to be put away. I found the small Galactic item and handed it to Dingus. "What is that, and is it safe to charge it up before we put it away?"

"It's an old style emergency beacon. I ran it 'til it went dead, by then I figured no one was coming. I gave it to her Grandpa, he liked the colors. I wouldn't bother charging it, she's got a better one now."

I put it in the pile to be put away. "Now the stuff I brought you down here for. All of her weapons have been sitting in that rusting car. We need to clean them up for her."

He picked up her little Colt. "This I pretty much understand, I think. I saw an Adams with that trigger cocking deal, back when. Most of this other stuff I've never seen, Bob."

"I can show you how they work. I saw how much skill you had when you worked over those Colts of yours. I need your magic touch to slick these up, better than new."

We worked our way through, sharpening knives, cleaning guns, Dingus slicking up where he could. He said, "She carried a lot of firepower, for just running around."

"The way I heard was that her first husband wouldn't let her keep guns in the house, so her car became her gun safe."

"He's the one let that boy grow up not respecting his mother?"

"The same."

"Kinda wish he was still alive, so I could kick him around some."

"Yep. Dee didn't deserve any of that."

We finished, and loaded everything, ready to be put away. Then we cleaned up. Topper came over, carrying a Frisbee. He asked, "This, sir, is a Frisbee. Would you like instruction in its operation?"

"I would, ZZ, I mean Topper."

Topper showed him how it was done, and we all had a rousing game, 'til my phone rang. It was Nikki. "Hey, Caveman, you guys about done with your man talk? Its getting to be lunch time."

"Oops, sorry, we were teaching Dingus the Frisbee. Be right up."

"My Grandpa, the serious gunslinger, playing Frisbee? Oh my. Caveman, you mess with everything you touch, don't you?"

"You could've picked a different garage, you know. It's as much your fault as mine."

"I don't buy that for a minute, Caveman. One of these days I'm gonna catch you with those contacts out!"

"Love you, Space Cadet. Be there in a minute."

"Love you, too, asshole."

We went up to the house and washed up for lunch. Dee walked by and sniffed. "Hoppe's number 9, my favorite aftershave. We going to the range after paintball, boys?"

Dingus spoke, saving me. "Something like that, D-lightful. It's a surprise, you wouldn't want to spoil it, would you?"

"You know I would, Space Ranger. What have you boys been up to?"

"Playing with ZZ, oh crap, I mean Topper and his friends. What's that thing called, Bob?"

"A Frisbee, Dingus."

"That's it, playing Frisbee with Topper and Taz and, oh, Bob, who's the other one?"

"Ozzie."

"I'll get their names straight. I'm just used to calling them by their numbers."

I said, "You're doing better than me. I was just saying 'hey robot', 'til I named them."

Dee said, "You boys are up to something, and you're not going to get me sidetracked that easy."

Joanna spoke up, "It's a good surprise, Delilah, I promise you that. Those boys have your best interest at heart, you know. Let them have their fun."

"All right, but I got my eye on you two bozos. Least John ain't here. That would be too much ornery in one place."

I said, "You're in for a treat, then. Not just the regular bunch is coming for paintball, your buddy Mike is gonna be there, too."

"My buddy? You mean that sergeant that hit on me? Bob, you're E-ville!"

"He's all right, I just hope he brings some fresh drawers for after he meets Colonel Dingus."

Nikki exclaimed, "Grandpa, you got promoted?"

Dingus said, "Courtesy promotion, when I retired, no biggie."

I asked, "So are you two hanging around then?"

"Probably, Why do you ask?"

"Well, there are a couple more places in the holler here we should probably buy up, just for security's sake. No use of 'em sitting empty. John's buying Shady Oaks, figured Dee would be a good choice to get it squared away. I could dang sure use some adult supervision, if you're up for it. You need more reasons? We just like having you around, and we miss you when you ain't."

"Well, Bob, since you put it like that, I think we could see our way clear to hang around for a spell, don't you, D-lightful?"

"Depends on this surprise you boys got going. I still don't trust you two."

I said, "At least she's still got good sense."

Dingus replied, "There is that. Hey, Bob, I've got a package for John. Could we take it on your truck?"

"Not a problem, but we may have to make two trips. I promised the boys paintball."

"You're a wonder, Bob Wilson. I nearly forgot, I know you said you didn't want to be paid for that teaching machine fix, but the Guide insists. Can I get your account info?"

"I suppose. Who would have thought just having dogs around would make so much difference."

Lyla spoke up, "Saved Genny's life."

Dee asked, "Who's Genny?"

Lyla said, "Leelee's Grandma."

Dingus said, "This Leelee would be the small human Taz was so fond of?"

I replied, "Sure is. She's a trooper. Her Grandma was passed out, and she couldn't hardly reach the controls, but she rigged it so Nikki could drive remote and bring them aboard the freighter."

"Sounds like Taz picked a good one for a friend."

"He did. Hope to see them sometime when there's not life on the line."

We finished up lunch, and the ladies piled in Nikki's rig to go to John's. I called the boys, and asked them to bring a maintenance bot and a few cans of foam. I backed the truck up to the barn, and the boys came over the hill, playing recorded instrumentals, and singing "That deaf, dumb, and blind bot, sure plays a mean paintball."

Dingus looked at me and said, "Those boys are something else. You ever get tired of saucer repair, you can take 'em on tour."

He showed them where the medpack was, and they put it in the truck. They jumped in beside it, and turned on their dog camo. Dingus said, "I knew this place was going to the dogs."

Taz faded his head in. "You will pay for that on the field of paintball, sir."

He faded back out. Dingus said, "These boys of yours take their fun seriously."

"They take it however they can get it. You should have seen when they got to go with us on a caper last night."

Taz faded back in. "Better than just holding the window, that's for sure." He faded out.

Dingus asked, "What?"

"He's talking about when we broke Joanna out of Shady Oaks. We tried to keep from leaving a trace, so the boys came along and took her window out of the frame and put it back when we were done. Made it a lot easier than dealing with paperwork."

We pulled in, and John was waiting on the porch. He stood and said, "I see you brought the Devious Dogs of Doom."

"They want to try paintball. As slow as they are over rough ground, I didn't think it would be that unfair."

"What's in the big pink box?"

"And your name is even John. Which one are you? John Smallberries?"

"Ouch, good comeback. Can we put that in the basement with the autodoc?"

Dingus looked confused. I said, "'Buckaroo Bonzai' in your culture pack."

"You boys!"

Snitz took a running leap from the porch and hit me chest high. I got the face lick supreme before I put him down. "I'm glad to see you too, Snitz."

The boys picked up the medpack and put it where John wanted. Then they went back to dog camo, and laid by the porch. Snitz was confused, and gave them a good sniff, but he laid down with them. People started trickling in, Julie dragging in last. I asked, "How is that restaurant going to run with the whole management team playing paintball? Can your highly trained staff make it a whole day by themselves?"

"Bob, you're an asshole. But you're right, I do have good people. Thanks to Joanna, I have time to give them the support they need to do even better. So, I guess I owe you, Bob, even if you are an asshole."

"John, it went by so fast I'm not sure, but was there a 'Thank you, Bob, for busting Joanna out of Shitty Oaks' in the middle there somewhere?"

"I thought I heard it too, Bob. Maybe we should hop in the autodoc and get our hearing checked."

"Yes, Bob, thank you. Is everyone here?"

"We thought we had a couple more people from out of town coming in, but we haven't heard from them."

Snitz started to whine, and Ozzie grabbed his collar. I got up to open the garage and pulled out my comm. I dialed Mike. "Are you gonna let me work on that clunker while you're here so it doesn't scare my dog?"

"You'll have to ask the Ensign, it's her vehicle."

"I've got the garage open. Please set down inside and shut down your power core."

"Okay, Bob."

I kept my comm out, just in case the Ensign decided to be stubborn about killing her power.

The saucer slid in, set down and became visible. Shortly, I heard Ozzie call out, "All clear, Boss."

I put my comm away. Mike and the Ensign came out. "Mr. Wilson, let me present Ensign Tinally Whittum. Ensign, Mr. Wilson."

I said, "Call me Bob, until you know me well enough to call me asshole."

Julie called out, "I heard that, Bob, you asshole!"

"Respect is a wonderful thing, don't you think, Ensign?"

"Wouldn't know, I get none either. Call me Tinally."

"Any chance we could shorten that to Tina?"

"I suppose. What were you saying on the way in about fixing my saucer?"

"With a few dollops of mounting putty, we can keep the plumbing around your power core from rattling. That means no ultrasonic screech, and Snitz stays happy."

"How long would that take?"

"Let's ask my maintenance supervisor. Topper! Front and center."

One of the dogs ran across the driveway, until he got inside and let his camo fade. He stood up and said, "Yes, Boss?"

"We have here a noisy saucer. How long would it take to make a quiet one out of it?"

"Thirty minutes, tops, Boss."

"Good enough for you, Tina?"

"Yes, that would be fine. Your bots camouflage as dogs, Bob? Why?"

"Topper, could you get started, please? Tina, to answer your question, it makes it easier to take them out in public, large autonomous robots are not a common sight on this planet."

Ozzie and Taz grabbed the small bot and the foam out of the truck bed, and came running. Topper was already pulling fasteners out of the access panel. I said, "Let's go get you introduced to everyone."

Dingus met us on the way to the house. Mike froze up. He stammered, "Sir, I had no idea you and she were together. I..I intended no offense, Sir."

Dingus laughed, "Relax, son. I don't eat sergeants for breakfast, regardless of what you may have heard."

Tina asked, "Sergeant, who is this man?"

Mike replied, "Ensign, don't you recognize Major Dingolus Slongum, the famous lost Guide?"

Dingus said, "They gave me a bump to colonel when I went back and retired, but yes, I'm the Guide who's famous for getting lost."

Tina looked floored. "So Benikkious Slongum, that I helped question, is your daughter?"

"Granddaughter."

Tina fainted dead away. Only Dingus' reflexes kept her from falling.

I called out, "Hey John, got any more smelling salts?"

John ran up, "What happened, Bob? You fart?"

I said, "She just realized she helped mess with Dingus' family the other day. I think she took it hard."

John broke the capsule under her nose, and she roused. "Sir, I take full responsibility for my actions. Our questioning of your family and associates was completely out of line."

"Easy, little one. The way I hear it, your entire chain of command ordered what happened, and you're freshly commissioned. The responsibility isn't yours to take. Major Rottum was using Patrol assets for a personal vendetta. That will be dealt with well above your pay grade."

"I am sorry, sir. I knew it wasn't right, the way we treated these people, but I went along with it. A failure of personal ethics."

"Your first posting dropped you in a bucket of shit. No one could expect a green Ensign to square that away by herself. You could have really screwed up, like hitting on the Colonel's fiance", he said, grinning at Mike.

Nikki saw what was going on, and came over. "Tina, I didn't enjoy what you did, obviously. But I don't hold you responsible for something Major Rottum ordered. Please try to relax, we're here to have fun today. Unless, of course, my Grandfather turns it into another hard core training session."

Dingus said, "Well, Nikki, I do need to see if your man did his homework."

We wandered on to the porch, and people introduced themselves all around. Jack asked, "So, is this everybody? Can we get suited up now?"

I said, "I think so. The boys want to play, so we shouldn't start without them, but they don't have to suit up, and they should be done soon."

"What are they doing, Bob?", Julie asked.

"Fixing Tina's saucer so it doesn't upset Snitz. Oh, hey, I forgot. Do you have a training machine on that rig, Tina?"

"Yes, it's standard equipment. Why do you ask, Bob?"

"You want the headache fix while you're here?"

"Headache fix? What do you mean?"

Dingus spoke up. "Bob and my Granddaughter figured out how to fix the training machines so they don't give you that awful headache. Doesn't take long to do, and it makes training ever so much nicer."

"Wait a minute, the last time I was here, you were talking about muscle relaxers. This is something new?"

I said, "Mike, you give her the file on the training machine mods?"

"I thought I did, maybe I missed it."

Tina spoke up, "I saw that file, I thought it was just the muscle relaxers."

Dingus said, "No, Ensign, this is a real fix, that removes the cause of the problem. The Guide think they are miracle workers. Eventually, the Patrol will get with the program, but you have an opportunity to get ahead of the curve."

I said, "Feel free to look at the file and do the mods yourself if you don't believe us. I would think a young officer, just starting out, would have a lot of training to do."

Tina replied, "Yes, I do. I'll look at the file myself, though, if you don't mind."

"Not at all. Let's play."

Choosing teams took a little bit, with so many people. Dingus and I were team captains, by popular demand. Dee was on Dingus' team, and Nikki on mine. Dingus got Taz, and I got Topper and Ozzie. I got John, and Dingus got Mike and Tina. Joanna wanted to be with Dee, and Julie wanted to be with Joanna. Jack went with them, and I got the rest of the regulars. I put the boys wide out on our flanks, and told them to move as quietly as they could. We started through the woods toward where the other team's flag had to be. We were spread out, advancing cover to cover, trying to find the other team. John saw a flash off to our left, dropped and rolled behind cover, yelling for everyone else to get down. NotherBob, Jacob, and Ozzie were tagged before we realized we were being sniped from above. Nikki found Taz poking out above the trees. He had used his extension legs to improve his firing position. She motioned to the rest of us, and Taz got a new paint job. I didn't hear the twig snap behind me in time to roll over and face the rest of Dingus' ambush. Nikki and John saw me move and were able to return fire. Jason tried to reach cover, but Dingus tagged him before he made it. Topper came running in, firing from the "hip", with good accuracy. He managed to hit Mike, Tina, and Joanna before Dingus put a stop to his charge. That left Nikki and John standing off Dingus and Julie. Dee was nowhere to be seen. She apparently had been Taz' security, because she came slipping in from that direction. She clocked Nikki and John before they realized she was there. We went back to reset, and to give Dingus' team a chance to rub our noses in it. Dingus said, "I want to review a few things with Mike and Tina", and then Dee started "Do do do, Proud Mary", and everybody not from off world lost it. In the confusion of explaining why it was so funny to our guests, I saw Topper go into his concentration trance. He didn't alert me of any problems, so I assumed there was orneriness afoot. I did wonder what he was up to, but I wanted to be surprised with everyone else. We played a few more rounds, did a little better, but never beat the mighty Dingus. Snitz wandered out, and decided to help me. He led me to Taz' hiding place, and I was able to get him and Dee before they sprang the ambush. That round ended in a draw, as Dingus and I shot each other at the same time. My team decided that was probably as good as we were going to do, and it was getting towards suppertime anyway. When we all got back to the house, John said, "Oh, Dee, I almost forgot. Your new ID came while you were gone. I'll get it for you." When he returned and gave her papers, she said, "Dee Sloan, I can get used to that."

John replied, "I figured it was as close to Slongum as I could do without it looking hinky."

Dee hugged him. "Thanks, John."

I said, "Anybody want to see the new shop the boys built me? From nothing to a completed building in under a week. These guys are a wonder."
Tina said, "Is there a place I can park over there? I'd rather be able to leave when we get done."
I said, "There's still room for one more in the barn, I'll open it when I get there and give you a call."
She said, "Anybody want to ride with us?"
Everyone who hadn't ridden in a saucer yet said, "Yes!", and they took off toward the garage. Topper motioned the rest of us to follow. Even Max was curious what was going on. When the garage door came up, we could all see the "nose art" Topper had given Tina's saucer. Below a nice picture of a steamboat, there was a script logo "Proud Mary". Tina said, "OH! My goodness, what is this? It's beautiful! Who did this? Topper came forward, and said, "I designed it, and programmed the maintenance bot to apply it. I hope it meets your approval, ma'am."
She hugged Topper and said, "You silly bot, it's wonderful! Thank you!"
After Topper explained he hadn't used paint, it was an anodizing process that would stand up to heat and wear, Tina was even more impressed. "This place is wonderful. I can't wait to come back."
I called, "Okay, boys, load up, let's go get the shop ready to show off."
Four dogs charged across the driveway and jumped into the truck. Snitz had found his pack.
Dingus said, "Mind if I ride with you, Bob??"
"Nope. Climb in."
I dropped Dingus off to open the barn, and drove the boys to the shop. They pushed the Chevelle out next to the door and handed me the keys. Topper had fabbed up a ZZ Top keychain. I heard John and Nikki pull in up at the house, and soon everyone was trooping down over the hill, with Dee in the lead. When they arrived, Dingus asked, "You sure you're ready for this, Son?"
"Ready as I'm gonna get, Sir."
I hit the button to run the door up, and the boys cut down on 'Bitchin' Chevelle'. Confused looks ran through the crowd, until the door got high enough for Dee to see what was on the other side. Snitz has hit me with a flying leap to the chest before, but I wasn't expecting Dee to do likewise.
"You found it! You wonderful man!"
"I did, but this isn't it. I couldn't buy the original, but I built you a new one from scratch."

She slid off me, looking dejected. "So it's not really my car?"
"It's as close as I could get. Check the taillight, if you don't believe me."
Her brow gathered, and she walked to the back of the car, to pull the taillight out on its hinge. I saw her face light up when she felt the holes she had drilled in the stock of the shotgun to make it easier to pull out of its hiding place. She drew it and looked at the serial number. She looked at me and said, "How?"
"We stole your stuff back last night. I took it by to show Joanna after we thought we had it finished, and she told me about you having a bunch of stashes. We scanned it, so we could build all the compartments, and went back after the stuff last night."
She held her shotgun close to her face and sniffed, "That's what you two were doing this morning. Cleaning my guns!"
"Put in fresh ammo, too." She racked the round out of the chamber, and caught it in the air. "Dang! Even the same loading I used to use. You're good, Bob!"
"Never do a vast thing in a half vast way."
"Don't tell me you did this wonderful paint? I thought the original was pretty, but this is just gorgeous!"
"I did almost no work at all on this. The boys did everything. Straighter and stronger than Chevy ever thought about. Topper did the paint."
"Where is Topper?"
"Who do you think is in the band?"
I guess the music just then struck her. "They made up a song, and everything? Damn, Bob! You and your boys know how to show a girl a good time!"
She put the shell back in the shotgun and put it away. "So I'm guessing it's a little different under the hood, too?"
"I went the lazy way, put in an LS instead of your old Big Block. It's still a 427, though. Gave you a couple extra gears, and the suspension you'll have to feel to believe. It handles."
"So does it have any power?"
"Look at the floor."
She looked at the rubber I had laid the other day. "You laid this without getting pushed out of shape? I didn't know you were that good a driver, Bob."
"I'm not. It's that suspension I was talking about."
She looked down, "Okay, I see plates, does she have insurance?"

"Sure does." I threw her the ZZ top keyring with her keys on. Suddenly, the bassline of the song cut out. Ozzie came across the floor full tilt. He stopped in front of Dee, and said, "Ma'am, please do us a favor?"
"What's that, Ozzie?"
"Drive her hard! She's built to run. If you can break her, we can fix her better. Drive her hard!"
Dee hugged Ozzie, "I'll do my best, Ozzie."
Topper stood beside Ozzie. "Ma'am, is the paint acceptable?"
"No, Topper, it is not just 'acceptable'. It is fan-frikkin-tastic!, you silly bot!" She hugged him too. Taz wandered over and got a hug also. "Who wants a ride?"
The chorus of "ME!" must have rattled windows miles away.
Dee said, "Let's see. Tina, you and Mike are going to have to get back to base soon, right?"
Tina replied, "Yes, we are."
"Okay, you two get the back seat, and Joanna gets shotgun. Load up people, we don't have all night!"
She worked her way through everyone. Some returned with a perma-grin, and some looked a little shaky when they crawled out. Nikki and I hung back, since we had driven it already. Dingus figured he'd have plenty of chances, so he hung back too. Dee finished up with everybody else, and went to talk to Tina. Tina must have agreed to take people back to John's, because they all left in Proud Mary. Dee closed the barn and came back down to the shop. "You bunch ready for your ride?"
Dingus said, "Where we headed, D-lightful?"
"I know a barbecue place up the road a ways. My friend Barb runs it." I looked at Nikki and smiled. Nikki said, "No wonder she asked about the Chevelle we were hauling home. Small world!"
"I thought you said the boys built it from scratch, Bob?"
"They did. I bought that pile of rust over there in the corner for a clean title. We stopped at your friend's place on the way back."
Dee studied on that a minute. "Bought a whole car just to get good paperwork. Money has made you a dangerous man, Bob Wilson."
"Then why did you let the Guide throw a bunch more at me?"
"We did talk them out of the statue, Bob. Be thankful for what you've got. Dingus has shotgun, you two in the back."
"Can we drop Snitz with Max?"
Ozzie ran over. "Boss, we can care for the canine while you are gone. He will get plenty of exercise."

"Okay, Ozzie, remember to put him out some water. I'll feed him when I get back."

"No problem, Boss."

We all piled in, and Dee showed us the power of sideways. She said, "The old setup was fast, but with two more gears, this thing is ridiculous. How many horses has it got, Bob?"

"Right at 700. Figured that was good enough for starters. If you decide you need more, Ozzie will figure something out."

"I think I'm good for a while, Bob. You put all the keys and papers back where they were?"

"The boys put things away, but I'd surely be surprised if they got something out of pocket. Are you missing something?"

"Haven't had time to look. Just trying to get used to the idea having my ride back. How much trouble did you go to for this old girl?"

"Got shot at once, but we were in a saucer, nobody got hurt."

"Shot at? Who has my old car?"

"Carl Jackson. Joanna said he was a friend of William's."

"That no account bum. If he's got it, it's because William told him to keep it."

"He sure wants to. Priced it to me for a hundred thousand, and acted like he wanted to go for his shotgun when that didn't immediately run me off. Can't say he's one of my favorite people."

Dingus spoke up. "Bob Wilson, friend to all, met someone he didn't like? I didn't know that could happen."

"He did dislike me first, Dingus. Kinda like Major Rottum and his nephew."

"You did have another go around with the Major, didn't you?"

"We did. This time he sent his flunky, though. Some Captain, didn't get his name. Named him Torky in my head, but not out loud."

Nikki asked, "Torky?"

"He reminded me of Torquemada."

She went to her watch, and the front seat answered in unison. "The Spanish Inquisition, the Grand Inquisitor."

Then Dee said, "I can see how you didn't get it. Nobody expects the Spanish Inquisition."

I replied, "Spam for supper, you say?"

Dingus asked, "What now?"

I answered, "In the culture pack, under Monty Python."

Dingus looked it up. "Oh! I see. I missed a lot snoozing in the backyard. D-lightful, sweetie, I have a question. If Barb knows you, and knows your car, isn't she going to notice you're not quite as old as you should be?"

"Oh crap! I hadn't thought about that, Space Ranger. I was so excited about having wheels under me again, I didn't think."

Nikki said,"It's okay, Dee. We've all been having trouble trying to keep things quiet. We need to come up with a better system."

Dee replied, "I've got this wonderful ride the boys worked so hard on, and I can't show it off without causing a fuss. As problems go, this is a good one to have, but it still sucks."

I spoke up, "Dingus, what exactly are the regulations about using Galactic medical tech on 'primitives'."

He replied, "You're sneaky, Bob Wilson, I'll give you that. Yes, we could give Barb back a few years in return for not making a fuss. Would that suit you, D-lightful?"

"You boys take such good care of me! Of course that suits me."

We got to the restaurant, looked like the supper crowd was thinning out. Dee tapped the horn, and when she got a regular sound, she turned to me and said, "You and the boys missed a trick, Bob. It's supposed to play the first few notes of 'Girls Just Wanna have Fun'."

"Damn, Dee, we didn't know. I'll get Taz right on it. Anything else we missed?"

"Not that I've found yet."

Nikki and I went in first. Barb looked from us to the car, and said, "You two didn't tell me you knew Delilah! That car is great! Looks like you updated a few things, though."

"Just a little more power, a couple more gears, and better handling."

"How did you get it looking so good so fast? When you had it on the trailer, it was a rust bucket."

"That one still is. I bought it for a clean title to put on this one my crew built from scratch. Wanna ride?"

"YES! What kind of stoopid question is that?"

She followed us out, where Dee and Dingus were waiting by the car. Barb went from stunned, to perplexed, to hugging Dee all in the space of about ten seconds. "How? You're so young! What's going on?"

"Grab shotgun and I'll tell you all about it while I show you what Bob had his boys build for me."

"COOL!"

"Grab us a table. We'll be back in a few minutes."

The rest of us wandered inside, found a table, and ordered drinks. I called Taz and told him about the horn. He said, "Sorry, Boss. None of us thought to check that."

"I didn't either, Taz. Don't feel bad."

"Thank you, Boss. I'll go over the scans and see what we can do."

"Thanks, Taz."

I hung up the comm, and said, "I wonder if the horn just slipped Joanna's mind, or she set me up?"

Nikki said, "Taz will get it fixed, what does it matter?"

"How much crap Joanna deserves rides on the answer."

There was a tire screech as Dee J-turned into the parking lot. They came through the door, Dee smiling, Barb with the perma-grin. They came over to the table. Barb said, "Dee ordered for everybody. I'll go get it started."

She left for the kitchen, and Dee sat down. She said, "We're all good. I love that car, Bob. Sorry I gave you crap about the horn."

"Not a problem. Taz is on the case, we'll get it fixed for you. We just want it to be right. We just didn't think to check the scans of the horn."

"Come on, Bob, ease up. You boys built me my dream car, only twice as good, and all I can find to bitch about is the horn? I'd say your bunch did darn good. That paint is magnificent. You think Topper would do fingernails?"

"I imagine he would relish the challenge, knowing him."

Our supper came, and it was great. Conversation died as everyone focused on eating. Barb brought out pie. I said, "I don't know if I can get around that, Barb."

Dee said, "Oh, come on, Bob, it's waffer thin!"

"Mr. Creosote, now, am I?"

Dingus looked at me, curious.

I said, "Same place as the last one. Dee's on a Python kick tonight."

We finished our pie, and I went up to pay. Barb said, "Your money's no good here, Bob Wilson. You go on now."

"If you're sure, Ma'am. Wouldn't want to wrestle you over it. Nikki gets jealous, don't you know."

"Dee's right, it's a miracle your eyes ain't brown."

Barb followed us back to our place, and Dingus got her set up in an autodoc. My comm rang. "Yes Taz, what's up?"

"Boss, could you bring Mrs. Slongum and the Chevelle to the shop? I think I have the horn right, but I'd like her opinion."

"Sure Taz. Be right there."

I hung up and said, "Dee, come on, your horn is ready."

We drove around to the shop. Dee asked, "Where's Joanna?"

"I dunno. Nikki's ride is here, so her and Lyla must be around someplace. Probably went to bed early. I think Lyla's headed back tomorrow."

"Oh. That makes sense."

Taz ran the door up for us. Topper and Ozzie were playing Frisbee with Snitz. After we got out, Taz said,"Please listen." He had a small metal box, hooked to the refurbed horn from the junk Chevelle. He touched the power wire to a battery charger. The horn played the riff, with just enough cartoony 'General Lee' sound to make it right.

Dee hugged him, "Thank you, Taz. This makes the car complete."

"You're welcome, Ma'am. I'm just sorry we didn't get it right the first time."

"Don't be a silly bot. You boys did a wonderful job! Nobody mentioned I had a custom horn."

"If you have a little time, I will install it for you."

"That would be very nice, Taz."

He popped the hood, drilled two holes, mounted and wired the box in hardly any time at all. He closed the hood gently, and said, "All done, Boss. I think we need a new project."

"Problem for another day, Taz. We'll see what comes up tomorrow."

Dee drove out and headed back to the house. I collected Snitz and headed to the house. On the way, the sound of Dee's new horn drifted down over the hill. I smiled as I walked up the hill.

Printed in Great Britain
by Amazon